BOLTON
D0315619
BT 309049018

For my beautiful wife, Karen, and our wonderful son, Euan.

Kelpies is an imprint of Floris Books
First published in 2016 by Floris Books
Text © 2016 Mark A. Smith
Illustrations © 2016 Floris Books

Mark A. Smith and Darren Gate have
asserted their rights under the Copyright,
Designs and Patents Act 1988 to be recognised
as the Author and Illustrator of this Work
All rights reserved. No part of this book may
be reproduced without prior permission of
Floris Books, Edinburgh
www.florisbooks.co.uk

The publisher acknowledges subsidy from
Creative Scotland towards the publication
of this volume

MIX
Paper from
responsible sources
FSC® C117931

Also available
as an eBook

British Library CIP Data available
ISBN 978-178250-326-2
Printed & bound by MBM Print SCS Ltd, Glasgow

MARK A. SMITH

Illustrated by
Darren Gate

1.
THE WORLD'S
WORST SUPERHERO

It was a sunny Sunday afternoon in St Andrews and Murdo McLeod – like every other self-respecting schoolboy in Scotland – was watching TV.

Murdo's favourite show, 'Mighty Mutant Monkeys from Mars', had only just started, when it was suddenly and unexpectedly interrupted by an emergency news bulletin.

AN ENORMOUS, SCALY, PREHISTORIC, MAN-EATING, FIRE-BREATHING, COUNTRY-MUSIC-LOVING MONSTER HAS EMERGED FROM THE RIVER TAY AND IS ATTACKING DUNDEE CITY CENTRE!

the excitable reporter exclaimed.

THE POLICE ARE POWERLESS TO STOP THE CREATURE'S RUTHLESS RAMPAGE!

"Great leaping lizards!" Murdo gasped. "This sounds like a job for... ME!" He leapt heroically from the sofa, pressed his magic belly button and was instantly transformed into the unmistakeably average

"Now, where did I put my keys...?"

After finding his keys – and leaving a note for his mum to say he'd be home by teatime – Murdo was off, speeding across the silvery Tay... on the number 99 bus. Not the most awe-inspiring mode of transportation, sure, but Batmobiles don't grow on trees, people!

While we're waiting for Murdo to arrive in Dundee (he'll take a while to get there), now seems as good a time as any to give you the lowdown on how a scrawny little kid from St Andrews became the scrawny little super-hero known as

First though, let's make one thing crystal clear, because I don't want anyone entering into this epic tale of bravery, suspense and white-knuckle adventures with any misconceptions: Murdo is *not* your typical superhero. Most superheroes are impossibly good-looking men and women, built like Olympic athletes, as powerful as Greek gods, and totally fearless. Murdo, on the other hand, is small and sort of awkward looking. He's got skinny arms and legs, and I wouldn't use the word 'brave' so much as the words 'daft', 'half-baked' or 'just plain clueless'.

Oh, and his not-so-awesome origin story, the story of how he gained his powers, that's not the most glamorous of tales, either. Still, if all that hasn't put you off, then read on, my friend, and prepare to be dazzled by all sorts of derring-do and, um, other stuff.

Like many modern-day marvels, Murdo owes his uncanny abilities to a radioactive creepy-crawly. Unlike some of those more upmarket, Hollywood-blockbuster-style caped crusaders, however, our SLUGBOY wasn't bitten by some free-range, corn-fed, cream-of-the-crop super-insect that had been experimented on in some fancy, futuristic laboratory. No, Murdo swallowed an irradiated bug while mucking about in Callum Campbell's back garden. And it wasn't even a cool bug, like a spider or a warrior beetle. It was a fat, grotty SLUG that had rolled around in toxic waste (and some other unmentionables) before

RUDE.

7

meeting its undignified end at the back of Murdo's throat. You see, a week earlier, Callum had claimed that he'd tried slugs at a French restaurant one time, and that they'd tasted like barbeque-beef-flavoured crisps. Murdo hadn't been convinced, but he'd figured there only one way to find out for sure...

So yeah, not the most spectacular of beginnings, but that fateful day left Murdo with much more than just a horrible taste in his mouth. He soon discovered that he could slide up walls on his tummy faster than a speeding... um, well, he's pretty slow, actually. Most of the time he slides at a gentle walking pace, because he needs to contract his stomach muscles to move up and down surfaces and it's really tricky. In fact, the last time Murdo tried to go a little bit quicker he lost his grip halfway up the side of his house and fell head first into his mum's compost heap, which was as embarrassing, as disgusting and yes, as stinky as it sounds!

As for Murdo's other powers, you already know about the magic-belly-button-superhero-transformation thing, so that just leaves one more, and let's just say I've not exactly kept the best till last...

Now, I hope you're sitting down for this because what I'm about to tell you might just *blow your mind!* Then again, it probably won't...

You see, Murdo's other power is to... Well, if he concentrates *really* hard then... How can I put this nicely?

His skin gets kind of... SLIMY . You know, sort of moist and greasy, like when you rub sunflower oil between your fingers. Not that you ever *would* rub sunflower oil between your fingers, but if you did then it'd feel exactly like Murdo's slimy skin.

Sadly, Murdo hasn't yet found any practical use for this particular talent – in a recent internet poll it was actually voted one of the most useless superpowers of all time! – but he's sure it's *bound* to come in handy sooner or later...

Anyway, he's finally reached his destination, so back to the story!

2.

DISASTER
IN DUNDEE

Murdo was so excited at the thought of going on a proper superhero mission, and battling an actual, honest-to-goodness monster, that he hadn't been able to sit still the entire journey to Dundee. His bus came to a gradual, grinding halt down the road from the Overgate Shopping Centre, and as he stumbled off, buzzing with nervous energy, he pictured people filling the streets to celebrate his impending victory over his larger-than-life opponent. OK, so he hadn't given any thought to how he might actually defeat the towering tyrant, but Murdo wasn't one for sweating small details like that.

He dashed to Dundee City Square and slid up the side of the Caird Hall, the city's largest, most prestigious concert venue, for a better view of his surroundings. When he eventually reached the roof, however, Murdo was exhausted. Sliding up walls is hard work!

"Just need... a minute... to catch... my breath," he panted, "and then... then it'll be

TIME!"

Unfortunately, as he staggered wearily towards the front of the building, Murdo slipped in pigeon poo and bashed his head, nearly knocking himself out! (Thank goodness the Caird Hall has a flat roof, huh?)

And so our hapless hero lay there, dazed and confused and counting the cartoon stars flashing before his eyes, completely oblivious to an epic battle that was unfolding not twenty yards away in the city centre!

That's right folks, another group of superheroes had arrived to save the day and they were giving the scaly, country-music-loving monster a real run for its money. The beast thrashed its tail and roared, lava spewed out of its flared nostrils and deadly laser beams shot from its eyes, but the mighty heroes battled valiantly until they finally gained the upper hand!

Meanwhile, Murdo was in a daze. He'd drifted off to the Land of Nod, that magical place where your dreams live. He imagined he was the world's greatest-ever superhero. People adored him, looked up to him, idolised him, and all the girls fancied him, too! He even had his own fan club, the **MURDO-MAD MOB**, or **TRIPLE M** for short. Murdo was about to deliver his acceptance speech for yet another Nobel Prize, this time for 'Outstanding Contribution to Saving the World', when he was rudely awoken by a freezing-cold blast of water to the face.

"Argh! Where am I? What year is this? And why am I all wet?"

"*I'm* why you're all wet, you moron!" snarled an unfamiliar woman's voice. She didn't sound too friendly.

Once Murdo had come to his senses and wiped the water from his eyes, he was stunned to find himself face-to-faces with the country's coolest crime-fighters:

THE ADVENTURE SQUAD!

who are:

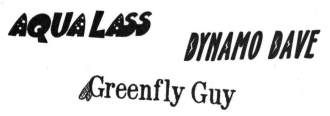

AQUA LASS

DYNAMO DAVE

Greenfly Guy

And the Squad's resident mind-reader:

PSYCHIC SALLY

Aqua Lass was the Squad's fearless leader, a stern, straight-talking taskmaster with a sharp tongue and an attitude to match. Her fingers were still dripping from soaking Murdo with her water-throwing abilities, and she looked decidedly unimpressed with the soggy sap sitting before her.

"I can't believe you slept through that whole battle." She waved a disapproving finger in Murdo's face. "And this isn't the first time you've slipped up, either! Don't look so surprised. We know all about your 'daring debut' at the community centre the other week."

"You heard about that?"

Aqua Lass scowled menacingly.

"In my defence," Murdo offered, "I thought those people were vandals about to graffiti the walls. They had paint cans and were wearing masks!"

"Those 'vandals' you courageously covered in slime were a bunch of little old ladies: charity workers who had volunteered to repaint the building. And the masks were to protect them from paint fumes. Any idiot could have worked that out."

"I didn't *cover* them in slime; it was more of a light coating. And I told them I was sorry—"

"Save it, slime bucket! You have some nerve calling yourself a superhero, pal! All you do is mess up and give the rest of us a bad name! You're an embarrassment. You should be ashamed to wear that cape."

This merciless barrage of insults continued until Psychic Sally came to Murdo's rescue.

"Don't be so hard on him, Aqua Lass," she said. "I'm sure Slugboy was just trying to help."

Aqua Lass didn't look convinced, but just when she seemed ready to launch into another hard-hitting rant, everyone's attention was drawn towards a weaselly little man that Dynamo Dave was holding in a headlock. He'd been there all along, but Murdo had been too starstruck to take any notice of him until now.

"Unhand me, you cumbersome Neanderthal," the man squealed, trying to wriggle free from Dave's vice-like grip. "You'll be hearing from my lawyers, you oversized imbecile!"

"Who *is* that?" Murdo asked, relieved to be out from under Aqua Lass's spotlight. "And what happened to that whopping big dinosaur thing that was attacking the city?"

"This is Brodie Bremner," Sally explained. "Better known around these parts as

BR●DIE BRAINWAVE."

"Of course it is!" Murdo had seen the sneaky super-villain on TV dozens of times, but hadn't recognised him in his swanky new costume. "So what diabolical evilness has the good-for-nothing lowlife been up to this time?"

"He was using his telepathic trickery to force that scaly, country-music-loving monster into attacking the city. Once we'd figured out what was going on, everyone else kept Godzilla-features busy while I tracked Brodie down and knocked him out with a heavy-duty mind-blast. It was all surprisingly straightforward."

"Awesome! And once he'd lost control of the creature...?"

"It moseyed on back into the River Tay. Turns out it's been living there peacefully for goodness knows how long."

"But I thought Brodie Brainwave could only control

small creatures, like rats and birds and those teeny-weeny dogs celebrities sometimes carry around in their handbags," Murdo said, recalling the description of Brodie's powers from his **Bottom Trumps Heroes and Villains** card game.

"He must have upgraded somehow." Sally shrugged. "Under normal circumstances I'd scan a villain's mind for more details, but Brodie's brainwave powers make him difficult to read, so unless he's feeling especially talkative..."

"Why don't you—"

"Enough!" Aqua Lass snapped, interrupting Murdo. "We have more important things to do than stand around here playing Twenty Questions with superhero-wannabes like you! Now come on, you lot." She took Brodie by the wrist and dragged him along behind her. "We'll drop this loser off at **THE SLAMMER** and then let's get back to base. Dave thinks he left the iron on again..."

"See you later, Slugboy," Sally called with a smile and a wink. "Keep on fighting the good fight!"

Aqua Lass shot Murdo one last scathing look before she and the rest of the Adventure Squad departed, leaving Murdo alone on the rooftop to reflect on his disastrous day...

"It could have been worse," he decided. "At least I got to meet the Adventure Squad. AND they've heard of me! How cool is that?!"

AQUA LASS (LEADER) — CONTROLS WATER, TRANSFORMS INTO WATER

Greenfly Guy — FLIES, HAS ENHANCED SENSES

DYNAMO DAVE — INCREASES HIS STRENGTH THROUGH PHYSICAL MOVEMENT

PSYCHIC SALLY — READS MINDS, MIND BLASTS, TELEPATHIC COMMUNICATION

Captain Scotland formed the Adventure Squad after being overwhelmed by his arch-nemesis, Major Disaster, and Disaster's robotic minions, the Deadly Dashing White Sergeants. Faced with a threat no individual hero could hope to conquer alone,

FORMER SQUAD MEMBERS INCLUDE:

CAPTAIN SCOTLAND, ARNOLD ARMSTRONG, THE GREEN LADY and THE GREAT SCOT

Captain S. banded together with Arnold Armstrong, Sir Sgian Dubh and the Green Lady to defeat Major Disaster and save the country.

The now government-funded Adventure Squad has become a national institution. They even have their own line of tasty pasta sauces; a particular favourite is Psychic Sally's Nutty Green Pesto! Nutritious and delicious!

The Squad's line-up has varied over the years and so too have their costumes. The most radical of their uniforms was an unfortunate black leather, punk-rock look adopted during a time-travelling mission to the 1970s. After agreeing that they looked more like a gang of bikers than a team of superheroes, the Adventure Squad dropped the leathers in favour of more traditional multi-coloured spandex outfits, and the world breathed a collective sigh of relief!

EVIL RATING 💀💀

<u>HEIGHT</u> (CM) — 178
<u>INTELLIGENCE</u> — 45
<u>STRENGTH</u> — 23
<u>SPEED</u> — 24

<u>FIGHTING SKILLS</u> —12
<u>COOKING SKILLS</u> — 84
(HE MAKES A MEAN
STIR-FRIED CHICKEN)

BIO

Picture this: it's a wet and wild night. Rain lashes down. Lightning crashes. Thunder rumbles. And Brodie Bremner crouches on his roof, fiddling with his satellite dish (not the brightest of sparks, our Brodie). And what happened next, well, it likely won't come as much of a shock to you...

Yep, Brodie was struck by lightning while clutching that poor old satellite dish. Getting zapped by one-hundred million volts didn't kill him, though. Instead it altered his grey matter so that he was able to tune his brainwaves to different frequencies, like tuning a TV or a radio to find new stations. Brodie found that by matching his brainwave frequency to that of an animal, he was able to influence and even control that creature's actions.

Naturally he used his newfound abilities to launch headlong into a life of super-crime, thus Brodie Brainwave was born!

TRIVIA

Brodie Brainwave tends to control small animals, as larger creatures require a far greater effort (and he's a bit of a lazy toad).

3.
BRIGHT LIGHTS
BIG ~~CITY~~
BADDIE

Murdo stepped off the train at Edinburgh Waverley Station the next morning with his chin up and his chest out. Despite his mishap in Dundee, he was feeling positive and looking forward to doing some crime fighting in the capital! There were bound to be some sinister scoundrels lurking nearby in a big city like Edinburgh, some vile villains in need of vanquishing.

Murdo had wanted to battle baddies here for ages, but to make his dream a reality he'd had to tell his mum that he and his friends were going to the zoo for the day. He didn't like lying to his mum, but he'd decided it was easier than having the whole awkward 'Mum, I'm a superhero' conversation.

Murdo's amazing plan for this morning was basically to ride the trams back and forth along Princes Street until a dirty-rotten-villain-who-was-up-to-no-good caught his eye. Then he'd explode into action and save the day, thus becoming renowned the world over as a top-notch superhero (and an all-round nice guy)!

Sadly, as the hours ticked by, the closest Murdo got to even a whiff of evil was the righteous stench coming from a sweaty jogger who didn't seem to believe in showering or in changing his smelly old socks.

Never one to be easily discouraged, however, Murdo decided it was time for **PLAN B!**

EW.

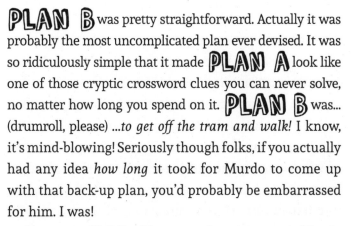

PLAN B was pretty straightforward. Actually it was probably the most uncomplicated plan ever devised. It was so ridiculously simple that it made **PLAN A** look like one of those cryptic crossword clues you can never solve, no matter how long you spend on it. **PLAN B** was... (drumroll, please) ...*to get off the tram and walk!* I know, it's mind-blowing! Seriously though folks, if you actually had any idea *how long* it took for Murdo to come up with that back-up plan, you'd probably be embarrassed for him. I was!

Anyway, still full of beans and raring to go, Murdo hopped off the tram and headed towards Charlotte Square. He passed plenty of punters out shopping and swarms of sightseers snapping away, but no baddies. He strolled along George Street, where the only criminal activity was some extremely dodgy parking. On and on he walked, past monuments, cafés, bars, expensive-looking houses and shops, all the while hoping to happen upon a heist or bump into a bank robber, but there was no sign of trouble. Undeterred, our valiant hero continued towards Rose Street, quietly humming the theme tune he'd recently written for himself, which goes a little bit like this (sing along if you know it, kids):

Here comes Slugboy, sliding up the wall!
Here comes Slugboy, looking brave and tall!
No matter where evil goes,
He will smell it with his nose!
Here comes Slugboy, here to save the day! Yay!

Catchy, innit?

Half an hour later an increasingly weary Murdo found himself on Edinburgh's historic Royal Mile, but sadly he was far too tired to enjoy his visit. His feet felt swollen and heavy, his legs were sore and tired, and his t-shirt was soaked with sweat. He was really thirsty, too, and his stomach was making all sorts of bizarre hungry noises, like a volcano that's about to blow its top.

But then, just as he was about to call it a day and go for lunch, Murdo spotted a super-criminal at last!

Well, he didn't 'spot' the villain, so much as he narrowly avoided being *stepped on* by him...

The first gigantic, metallic foot came crashing down where Murdo had stood only moments before, scaring the pants off him and sending shockwaves up and down the street. Passers-by screamed and scurried for cover as another enormous foot landed twenty metres further forward, trashing some traffic lights with a thunderous thump.

Each almighty foot was connected to a series of thick chrome cables that stretched high into the sky, weaving and coiling around each other to form the impossibly long lower limbs of the notorious

DADDY LONGLEGS!

"Great jumping jellyfish!" Murdo gasped. Longlegs was a classic Golden Age villain who'd had his sinister schemes thwarted by some of the best heroes in the business, and he was undoubtedly the most high-profile baddie Murdo had ever encountered!

Longlegs didn't have any superhuman abilities, but he wore a robotic suit that was incredibly powerful and which had ludicrously lengthy arms and legs. Up there amongst the clouds, the villain himself was only just visible, sitting inside his little transparent command centre, calmly guiding his massive motorised limbs onwards without giving a second thought to the freaked-out folks below.

As he watched the technologically enhanced outlaw marching along the street, Murdo actually felt a little starstruck. He looked on in awe as Longlegs took another humongous stride, this time bashing a building and flattening a lamppost. In all the news footage Murdo had poured over, in the dozens of newspaper clippings he'd stuck in his scrapbooks, in the comics he'd read and in the cartoons he'd watched, Longlegs had never looked so incredibly tall. Even the usually reliable stats on his **Bottom Trumps Heroes and Villains** card didn't do Longlegs justice – not unless he'd recently experienced some sort of gargantuan growth spurt!

Murdo was still staring at Longlegs, dumbfounded, as the mechanical menace disappeared into the distance.

"This is so cool," he said to himself. "And me without my camera!"

At that moment a ridiculously overdramatic damsel crossed Murdo's path, swooning and swaying and gesturing theatrically.

"Heavens!" the damsel called in her best Shakespearean voice. "Whatever shall we do? If only there were some brave soul out there, some daring champion, some super, amazing, totally awesome guy who could save us from that evil fiend!"

"You can say that again," Murdo muttered under his breath.

Yeah, I know what you're thinking.

Give him some time, he'll figure it out in a minute or two.

"Oh, wait just a second now," Murdo continued, as the penny finally dropped, "that's *me*! I'M the totally awesome, brave soul guy!"

Sliding up walls isn't the only thing he does slowly, folks...

Now that he'd realised that he was the totally awesome, brave soul guy – his words, not mine – Murdo scanned his surroundings for a private place where he could transform into **SLUGBOY** without compromising his secret identity. He made his way through the panicked pedestrians towards a nearby bar, Deacon Brodie's Tavern.

Entering the pub, Murdo found no evidence of the chaotic scenes unfolding outside. Nobody even looked up as the door slammed behind him. He strode across to the barman, a formidable-looking chap, big and burly with a bushy handlebar moustache.

"Where's the gents?" Murdo asked.

"Toilets are for customers only," the barman grunted without looking up.

"But this is an emergency!"

"You gonna have an accident?"

"What? No! That's not what I meant!"

"Look kid, I don't make the rules. You wanna use the facilities, you gotta order something. Otherwise quit wasting my time."

"Fine," Murdo said, exasperated. "I'll take a packet of cheesy Wotsits and a purple Fruit Shoot."

The barman smirked. "I'll need to see some ID."

"What?!"

"Can't sell you anything without seeing some ID, kid. Them's the rules."

"But all I want is some Wotsits! I mean, I don't even *want* Wotsits – I just need to use your bathroom! For two seconds!"

"Like I said, I don't make the rules."

"You know what? Forget it! I don't have time for this!" Murdo snapped as he stormed out with a face like fizz.

Outside the bar, Murdo found himself standing in front of two red telephone boxes. He regarded them with some scepticism. *It's a bit of a cliché*, he thought, *but I guess if it's good enough for the Man of Steel...*

Within seconds Murdo had emerged from the nearest telephone box in his Slugboy garb, much to the excitement of a passing group of children.

"Who's he supposed to be?" asked one of them, a tall scruffy girl.

"Ah dinnae ken," replied her friend. "Is he no the new mascot for the Hibees?"

"Naw," piped up another kid, "he's that boy off the advert, the loo paper one!"

"Oh aye, right enough! Here, do you reckon they're filming now? Maybe we'll be on the telly!"

OK, so maybe they weren't excited exactly (or if they were, it was for all the wrong reasons), but they were looking in the right general direction without laughing or throwing fruit, so that was good!

"Never fear, my friends!" Murdo bellowed in his most bombastic superhero voice. "Whilst evil yet lurks, the spectacular SLUGBOY shall oppose it!" And with that he launched himself up a lamppost, taking off like one of those rockets you make in science class with a plastic bottle and a bicycle pump. Except, you know, way slower and without the flying.

"What did he say?" asked one of the kids, as Murdo glided gradually upwards.

"Dunno," replied the scruffy girl. "Couldn't hear him over them police sirens. Probably something about loo paper," she guessed, before she lost interest and wandered off.

Daddy Longlegs was long gone by the time Murdo had slid high enough to survey the scene, but it was pretty clear which way he'd travelled, as the fiend had left a none-too-subtle trail of devastation in his wake.

Our hero was soon careering along the Royal Mile on a bicycle he'd found abandoned at the side of the road: a pink one with a basket on the front and ribbons on the handlebars. He sped past crumpled cars, squashed signs and mangled monuments, completely oblivious to how utterly ludicrous he looked. Superheroes are supposed to be stylish and smooth and make awesome, breathtaking entrances, like swinging into action without breaking a sweat, or pulling up in a state-of-the-art, billion-dollar stealth plane and announcing their presence with a wicked one-liner. Cycling to the rescue with your cape flapping limply behind you, your little legs pedalling furiously as your face turns redder than a sun-blushed tomato... Sorry pal, but that doesn't look cool at all, and it's hardly likely to strike fear into the heart of a tried-and-tested wrongdoer like *DADDY LONGLEGS*!

As Murdo trundled along unsteadily, trying desperately to avoid colliding with panic-stricken citizens fleeing in the opposite direction, the wide street gradually became narrower and distinctly 'older looking', until at last Edinburgh Castle loomed into view in all its resplendent glory (that's a posh way of saying it looks pretty awesome). And there, towering above the castle with his lanky arms flailing and his beady eyes glaring, was the dreaded *DADDY LONGLEGS*!

Murdo took a deep breath. "Finally," he said, "it's time for Slugboy to make a name for himself. Here goes nothing..."

4.
CAPITAL
CATASTROPHE

Murdo felt every inch the sensational superhero as he slid up and over the castle's high stone walls. He heard a chorus of imaginary trumpets blasting a bombastic fanfare in his honour, saw pretend paparazzi photographing his every move, and in his mind he signed dozens of autographs for his fictional fans.

"This is it," Murdo told himself. "This is my moment. This is my time to shine! Now, at long last, I'll make a name for myself and—"

"Oi!" called a coarse voice from below. "Ticket!"

"Sorry?" Murdo looked down to see a wiry little fellow standing outside the ticket booth.

"No entry to the castle without a ticket, mate," he said.

"You have *got* to be kidding me!"

"I'm not exactly known for my sense of humour, sunshine. Do you want a ticket or not?"

Murdo slid down the wall and along to the ticket booth. Normally the queue for the castle was long and looping, but the supervillain assault had frightened everyone away – so at least he wouldn't be kept waiting. Always looking on the bright side, our Murdo!

"Err, one concession, please," he said sheepishly. He felt a bit silly buying a ticket in his Slugboy costume. *Captain Scotland would* so *not have to do this*, he thought.

"Would you be interested in purchasing a copy of the official souvenir guide?"

Murdo stared at the man, flabbergasted. Then he eyed him suspiciously. "You don't have a brother who works at Deacon Brodie's Tavern, do you?"

"Not that I know of... Why?"

"You just reminded me of someone. Unless... Oh man, I don't have a sign taped to my cape that says waste my time again, do I?"

"Is that something that's happened to you before?"

"What? Oh, um... Never mind that just now, there's no time to lose!"

"It's only £3.99 when purchased alongside your ticket."

"What? What is?"

"The souvenir guide."

"Oh! Well, that does sound very reasonable... OK, fine, but be quick about it – I'm here to save the day!"

"I wouldn't worry about that, lad," the man said while he printed Murdo's ticket. "There's still an active barracks located within the grounds of the castle, next to the regimental museums. If anyone tries to cause trouble around these parts, the whole place will be swarming with soldiers before you know it."

"What?! No way! *Please* tell me you're joking..."

"Sorry sunshine, no sense of humour, remember?"

Moments later Murdo was zooming towards the castle gates at top speed (so not particularly fast, then), clutching his official souvenir guide, a look of grave concern etched across his fatigued face. It wasn't that he didn't want Daddy Longlegs stopped, it's just that he wanted it to be *him* who stopped the long-limbed lawbreaker, not some random military types! If the castle was already crawling with soldiers then he might as well kiss his moment of glory goodbye!

As it turned out, Murdo needn't have worried. After consulting the map in his official Edinburgh Castle souvenir guide, he arrived at the barracks to find the entire building bound by a writhing mass of metallic coils. The dastardly Daddy Longlegs had wrapped one of his ridiculously lengthy legs around the barracks, trapping all the soldiers inside!

The villain's other leg wasn't too far away, either. He was using it to detain all of the people visiting the castle who hadn't managed to escape upon his arrival. He'd corralled them together like a herd of sheep and imprisoned them inside St Margaret's Chapel, twisting his leg around the exits to prevent anyone from escaping.

"At least with both of his legs tied up here, Longlegs won't be going anywhere anytime soon," Murdo noted.

He followed the robotic legs up a steep, cobbled walkway and around the corner into the castle's Crown Square: a large, open courtyard, home to the Royal Palace, the Great Hall, the Scottish National War Memorial and, err... a tearoom, actually! It's a very nice tearoom, but it does seem a bit out of place... Anyway, it was here in Crown Square that Murdo finally found his fearsome foe, and he was pleased to note that, up close, Longlegs wasn't half as scary as he'd expected him to be.

With his mechanical legs fully extended and occupied elsewhere, Longlegs was left bobbing awkwardly about one metre off the ground, inside what looked like an enormous see-through egg. Despite being best known for his long limbs, Longlegs was actually a short, stout man, with a round belly and a big bald head. Sitting in his egg, with his dumpy little arms and stumpy little legs working furiously at the swirling mass of flashing lights, levers and pulleys, Longlegs reminded Murdo of a baby in a bouncy chair, one with lots of activities to keep the wee tyke entertained.

Longlegs hadn't actually noticed Murdo yet because he was glued to one of the screens in his egg. Not literally glued, because that'd be weird, but he was staring intently at it, as if in a trance. One of his long mechanical arms, meanwhile, was reaching across the courtyard and into the entrance to the Royal Palace.

This is too easy, our heroic protagonist decided. *He's not got the use of his legs, which are, let's face it, his main claim to fame and his most potent means of attack. And while he's reaching into the palace like that he might as well have one arm tied behind his back. This'll be like taking candy from a baby! A big, ugly, evil baby!*

Murdo couldn't contain a little chuckle. Confronted with his first major supervillain, all he could think about was how much the guy reminded him of a teeny, tiny toddler.

Sadly that self-same toddler lookalike had fantastic hearing and, without warning, a massive mechanical hand swept in from the side, viciously swatting Murdo clean off his feet and sending him crashing into a wall!

5.
CASTLE CALAMITY PART ONE

Murdo's head was spinning. His arm throbbed and felt as though it might be broken. He swayed and stumbled as he tried to regain his footing.

"This stinks," he complained. "Heroes on TV – *OUCH!* – never get injured!"

Murdo instinctively started sliding up the outside wall of the Great Hall, where he had landed after being battered by the giant robo-hand, but Daddy Longlegs slammed him back down to the ground with a sickening crunch.

"Oh man, I'm so going to feel that in the morning!"

"You needn't worry about feeling anything ever again, child," Longlegs sneered in a high, nasal voice. "You won't be able to once I'm through with you!"

Longlegs raised his huge robotic fist high into the air, ready to unleash a mighty hammer blow that would surely crush our fledgling hero and bring his short crime-fighting career to a sudden, painful end.

"Wait!" shouted Murdo. "Don't you want to know who I am?"

"Honestly? I couldn't care less about who you are," Daddy Longlegs scoffed.

"Well gee, that hurts almost as much as my broken arm, but OK… err, oh, aren't you going to explain your devious plan before you squash me? Baddies *love* explaining their devious plans!"

"And I suppose after that you'd like me to slowly lower you into a shark-infested pool while I make my getaway, hmm? Or is there some other ridiculous situation you'd rather escape from, eh? Please, child, I'm not some cheesy, moustache-twiddling, cliché-riddled villain plucked from out of a 1960s comic book," Longlegs said, twiddling his moustache. And on that note, his fist fell.

"Wait! Wait!" Murdo pleaded again, sounding slightly more panicked this time.

The fist froze a mere metre from flattening him.

"Just one last thing," Murdo begged, "and then I promise not to interrupt again."

"Ha! You say that like you have some choice in the matter." Longlegs's fist hovered ominously over his mismatched opponent. "Make it quick, boy. I'm on a tight schedule."

"Right, so, first of all, thanks for not squashing me yet. And I mean that from the heart. Secondly, and I know this will sound weird because you're going to be killing me shortly, but it's really cool to meet you! You're actually one of my top ten favourite villains of all time, and under different circumstances I might have been tempted to list all ten of them, but I can see you're busy so this maybe isn't the best time..." Murdo gulped as Longlegs turned his robo-arm slightly to glance at his humungous wristwatch. "Um, anyway, onto that one last thing..." he continued. "So, you know that Scottish superhero, the really muscly one with the spiky blonde hair and the big red 'A' on his costume?"

"Yes..."

"Cool. Um... I was just wondering... what's his name again?"

"That's your 'one last thing?'"

"Yep, it sure is! So... do you know what he's called?"

"Of course I know what he's called! *Everyone* knows what he's called! That beefy bonehead's called **ARNOLD ARMSTRONG!** But why on Earth, in the final few moments of your worthless, misbegotten life, would you ask such a trivial question?"

Murdo smirked. "Because he's right behind you, **BIRDBRAIN!**"

Daddy Longlegs didn't know what hit him. Well, he did actually, but only because Murdo had told him in advance! The villain turned to see a fast, furious fist flying towards him, a fist that connected sweetly with his giant egg and sent him hurtling across the courtyard. That crushing impact heralded the timely arrival of Arnold Armstrong, the world's mightiest man! And now Longlegs was in for a world of hurt...

Armstrong glanced over to Murdo. He looked concerned.

What a guy, Murdo thought. *Here he is, faced with a deadly enemy, and his first thought is to check that I'm alright...*

Though his battered body ached from head to toe – he felt as though he were a walking bruise – Murdo called, "Don't worry about me, I'm fine!" He wanted to add, "Sign my cape!" but resisted that urge. *Can't go round asking for autographs from every super-person I meet, not if I want to be taken seriously. Besides, I don't have a pen with me...*

Arnold took a few heroic strides towards Murdo, his eyes darting back and forth, making sure that creep Longlegs was down for the count.

Murdo held his breath as the chiselled champion approached. The next words out of Arnold's mouth could be life changing. Maybe he would say, "I need your help to defeat Daddy Longlegs," or "You must be that SLUGBOY I've heard so much about!" Murdo felt dizzy. His mind was spinning with possibilities, each as unlikely as the next, but no amount of hypothesising could have prepared him for what Arnold actually said...

Before we find out what those momentous words were, though, let's take a moment to consider just how important a figure Arnold Armstrong actually is, shall we? Yes, dear readers, it's time for a super-speedy, super-fun superhero history lesson! Yahoo!

Arnold has been around for years. He was one of Scotland's first superheroes and a founding member of the original Adventure Squad. He's averted alien invasions single-handedly and saved many a fair maiden from all manner of unsavoury ends. Arnold was also the first hero in the UK to secure corporate sponsorship, allowing him to quit his day job as a florist to fight evil full-time. He's the main character in a highly successful, fully licensed animated series and has been made into an awesome action figure that has real lights and sounds, a range of exciting accessories and thirty-three points of articulation. Thirty-three!

All very impressive, I'm sure you'll agree, but more important than any of that, Arnold Armstrong is actually the reason Murdo decided to become a superhero in the first place. He's Murdo's inspiration, his role model, the person he most wants to be like when he's older, so I'm sure you can appreciate that his first words to Murdo are bound to be a big deal to our daring do-gooder.

And those all-important words are...

"How's my hair? Is it OK? Is it a mess? It's a mess, isn't it? I knew it!"

Murdo was bamboozled, and that's not a word I use lightly! Surely his idol hadn't just asked about his *hair*, of all things? Not when there were innocent lives at risk?! Maybe Murdo had misheard. Maybe he was concussed after being walloped against that wall. Maybe he was hallucinating or delirious or something. Unfortunately, as Arnold went on, this seemed less and less likely to be the case.

"It's just that I came straight from a photoshoot for next year's *Arnold's Amazing Abs Calendar*, so I haven't had a chance to check!"

"Check what?"

"Uh, my hair of course! Try to keep up, eh?"

Murdo had no idea how to respond to this. Arnold had always come across as such a noble, selfless character on TV, the quintessential superhero if ever there was one, but this... Murdo wasn't sure *what* to make of this.

"So who are you anyway?" Arnold asked, checking out his reflection in a nearby window and then getting completely distracted by it. "Actually, it's not bad," he said, running his fingers through his hair. "Not bad at all..."

"I'm SLUGBOY," Murdo said, trying to sound impressive.

"Come again?"

"Slugboy," Murdo repeated.

"Really?"

"Really."

"You pick that name yourself or did you lose a bet?"

"Sorry?"

"Never mind. Who are you here with, kiddo?"

"Uh, I'm not sure I understand the question..."

"Ah, I get it – you're a bit on the slow side! Right, let me try that again, but this time I'm going to say it *verrrry slooowly*. Who – is – your – boss? I'm assuming you must be someone's comedy sidekick, otherwise why would you be dressed like that?"

"Dressed like what?" Murdo asked.

"Wow. Look kid, this has been fun, really it has, but let's get it over with as quickly as possible, yeah? I have a spray tan appointment booked for this afternoon and I don't want to be late. Just try not to get in my way."

Murdo was speechless, disappointed, embarrassed and slightly insulted all at the same time. His mind raced with a hundred possible comebacks, but his tongue got all twisted up inside his mouth and nothing came out. Luckily Daddy Longlegs cut their conversation short anyway. And when I say he cut their conversation short, what I mean is that he took hold of Arnold's ankles in his one free hand, swept him up off the ground and started swinging him round like a lasso, thumping him against the castle walls.

Murdo launched himself at Longlegs, but his attack was short-lived. The villain batted him out of the air mid-leap, using Arnold as a club.

"Let him go, you flabby fiend!" Murdo cried as he braced himself for another assault.

"Now hold on just one second," Longlegs huffed. "I'll have you know I'm actually very sensitive about my weight and I think that you, a so-called 'superhero', should be above such cruel petty name-calling. What sort of example are you setting to your young impressionable fans? You should be ashamed!"

And suddenly Murdo *did* feel ashamed. "You're right," he said, "and I'm sorry. I should know better than to—"

THWACK!

That, my friends, was the sound of Longlegs pounding Murdo over the head with a superhero. He thumped, clobbered, thrashed and pummelled him... and this time Murdo didn't get up. His vision went dark and fuzzy. His head hurt like blazes. And he was vaguely aware of laughter. Not nice laughter, like you hear at children's birthday parties. This was evil laughter, the kind you hear when a mean kid plays a trick on his unsuspecting little brother, or someone drops their tray in the dinner hall and everyone claps and cheers.

He played me, Murdo realised, clinging onto consciousness. *Rotten old wart probably doesn't give two hoots about his weight*, he concluded, and then he blacked out.

When Murdo came to, he was propped against a bench outside the War Memorial. Longlegs was still in the middle of Crown Square, looking awfully pleased with himself, but Arnold was nowhere to be seen.

"Looking for this?" Longlegs asked, raising his arm. He'd wrapped his coils around something big and broad, creating a sort of colossal chrome chrysalis.

"Arnold!"

"Come any closer, boy, and I'll crush the life out of this muscle-bound knucklehead faster than you can say, 'Red lorry, yellow lorry, red lorry, yellow lorry.'"

"What? Why would I say that?"

"It's a tongue twister. It's famous."

"What's a tongue twister?"

"Honestly, child, don't you know *anything*?"

"Um..."

"You know what, don't answer that, just listen, because if you don't do exactly as I tell you then I'll squeeze old Arnold what's-his-face here like a zit, until he goes pop like the weasel – and it'll be all your fault!"

"What do you want from me, Longlegs?" Murdo asked defiantly.

Longlegs had a ghastly glimmer in his eye and grinned the most nefarious grin ever grinned by anyone who's ever grinned.

"Why, you're going to help me steal the crown jewels, of course!"

6.
CASTLE CALAMITY
PART TWO

Edinburgh Castle's Royal Palace was once home to kings and queens, like Mary Queen of Scots and David II, son of Robert the Bruce. Later, the military used it for nearly two hundred years. These days it's a museum, chronicling the lives and times of the Scottish aristocracy.

Usually the palace was stuffed full of visitors, but right now Murdo had the place to himself. As he slid along the walls of the narrow, dimly lit corridors, he couldn't help but be creeped-out by the life-like waxworks that populated the passageways and by the deathly silence.

"Keep going, Murdo," our fledgling superhero told himself. "Arnold's relying on you!" Yes, folks, Arnold Armstrong's life was in Murdo's hands. That's a whole lot of pressure to put on someone, when you think about it, and sadly Murdo had never done particularly well under pressure. His neighbours once asked him to look after their pet rabbit while they were away on holiday. Murdo not only lost Mr Snuggle-Buddy-

Wiggle-Pants*, he also managed to cut down a two-hundred-year-old tree and explode his mum's microwave while searching for the bothersome bunny! Then there was the morning Murdo was running late for a maths test: his whole school had to be evacuated and the coastguard was called in to investigate reports of a masked man scaling the walls of the building while dressed in Spongebob Squarepants pyjamas and fluffy slippers... But that's a story for another time!

So yeah, Murdo + pressure = not so good!

Despite that, Murdo's mission in the Royal Palace had more or less gone according to plan so far, which was nice. Then again, the mission was to steal Scotland's crown jewels for a notorious villain, so maybe that's not so nice after all.

Back in the courtyard, Longlegs had explained to Murdo exactly how to nab the jewels, and had told him that if he didn't deliver the loot on time that Arnold was as good as dead. Murdo was now following the villain's stupendously stretchy artificial arm through the palace's claustrophobic corridors and up the tight winding staircases, wracking his brain (not as painful as it sounds, by the way), trying to concoct a way to rescue Arnold *without* handing over the crown jewels.

Time, however, was against Murdo. Before long he

* Warning: Do NOT let five year olds name their pets – it never ends well for anyone, least of all for poor old Snuggle-Buddy-Wiggle-Pants!

entered a big bright room that he immediately realised was the entryway to the crown jewels display. Longlegs's king-sized fist had already taken care of the two butch security guards, who were now slouched against each other on the floor, barely conscious and groaning quietly, their bashed heads lolling from side to side. The great mechanical fist hovered above them menacingly, silently gesturing towards a large locked door in the corner of the room.

As Murdo tottered uncertainly to the door, stepping over the security guards, he cast his mind back to his recent conversation in the courtyard.

"When the castle's silent security alarm is triggered," Longlegs had explained, "the vault containing the crown jewels automatically goes into lockdown. The only way to unlock it is to enter a code in two different locations simultaneously."

"Simul-what now?"

"At the same time," Longlegs had sighed.

"Ah. Couldn't you just have said that?"

Longlegs simply scowled and applied more pressure to Arnold in response.

"OK, OK, I'm sorry, stop it already!"

"I had planned on entering the codes myself, but I can't fit both of my arms into the building through that tiny doorway and I'm somewhat reluctant to damage a national treasure such as Edinburgh Castle."

"A villain with principles, eh? Good for you, Longlegs! But you do realise that the crown jewels are national treasures, too, right?"

"Yes, but I'm not intending on damaging those, either. I'm going to *steal* them."

"A good point well made. In that case, and this is probably a silly question, but can't you just smash your way into the vault? Or is that a national treasure as well?"

"The vault was designed to withstand a direct hit from a nuclear warhead, child. The walls are half a metre thick and made of reinforced graphene, the strongest metal known to humankind. They're also charged with enough electricity to charbroil anyone who tries to gain access without first entering the code."

"A simple 'no' would've been fine," Murdo mumbled.

"Enough!" Longlegs had finally snapped. "I have neither the time nor the patience for this nonsense! Now, memorise these instructions or prepare to bid Armstrong a fond farewell!"

Standing before the vault door, remembering Arnold's muffled yells from beneath those thick metal coils as Longlegs had tightened his grip, Murdo knew he couldn't afford to mess this up! One of the barely conscious guards had a key card hooked on a chain round his neck. Murdo took the card and swiped it along the edge of the door. A hidden panel on the wall slid open, revealing a small keypad of softly glowing digits. That was the cue for Longlegs's great fist to leave the room and speed towards the other keypad, located in the castle's deepest, darkest dungeon.

Murdo glanced at his Lego Batman watch. Longlegs had instructed him to enter the code and then press

at precisely 2.00 pm, to ensure they hit the buttons here and in the dungeon simelltan... somulten... at the same time. That gave him about three-and-a-half minutes to try and remember the code.

Unfortunately, Murdo didn't have much of a memory for figures...

When Longlegs had told him the code for the vault door, Murdo had tried to match each of the five digits to a different image in his head. Someone clever had taught him to do that a few years ago, but he couldn't remember who... It's a shame he didn't have a pen on him – it would've been much easier to just write the code down on the back of his hand (and then he could have got Arnold Armstrong's autograph, too).

At least the first number of the code was easy. It was three, for three musketeers, three little pigs and three sides to a triangle. It was also how many times Murdo had needed to re-sit his most recent maths test, but he made me promise not to mention that... Oops!

Next was the number six, for which Murdo had pictured his Great-uncle Albert's fingers, because he only had six of the ten left; he'd lost the other four in various toaster-related accidents over the years. Not the sharpest tool in the shed, old Albert, but he does love his toast!

Then it was a seven after that, definitely, for seven days in a week, Seven Wonders of the World and for S Club 7, a cheesy pop group from the late nineties. Not that Murdo particularly liked S Club 7, of course, but his mum used to have their CD in the car and listened to it whenever she was reminiscing about the old days (which was quite often).

Murdo was pleasantly surprised at how well he was remembering all this.

Way to go, me! he thought. And then, just as he was about to give himself a hearty pat on the back, things took a slight turn for the worse.

He had two more numbers of the five-digit code to think of. Those numbers were four and five. Four for the four oversized wheels on the green monster truck he'd ridden during a visit to Truckfest Scotland. Five for the five tiny planets left on Granddad's model of the Milky

Way after Great-uncle Albert had swallowed the rest of them to win a bet.

Yep, it was four and five all right... but which came first? Was it five and then four, or four then five? Wheels and then planets, or planets then wheels, or...

"Aw, nuts."

Murdo looked at his watch anxiously. It was 1.59 pm. There were only thirty seconds to go! His hand trembled as he pushed three–six–seven... and then his mind went completely blank, as if all of his thoughts and memories had suddenly been sucked into a great empty void of nothingness and vanished without a trace, never to be seen or heard from ever again! For a moment or two he even forgot which numbers he had to choose between.

Twenty seconds...

"Four and five," Murdo told himself. "Wheels and planets... That's got to be it! Unless of course it's not... *Ay, caramba!*"

Ten seconds...

Murdo's tummy tightened. The blood drained from his face. Sweat trickled down his cheek and he suddenly felt light-headed. He started picturing planets on wheels, which wasn't helping anyone!

Seven... six...

White lights danced before his eyes. His legs turned to jelly and battled to keep him upright.

Come on, Murdo, you can do this.

Three... two... one...

It was now or never. Murdo squeezed his eyes shut, bashed four and five at the same time and slammed the button, hoping for the best.[**]

...zero.

[**] Warning: This is *probably* not the most scientific method and I would strongly advise against this approach should you ever find yourself in a similar situation.

7.
CASTLE CALAMITY
PART THREE

Murdo peeked out from between his fingers. Nothing seemed to be happening. He hadn't been electrocuted, which was good, but the door to the crown jewels hadn't budged either, which wasn't so good. Normally when Murdo messed up (like he'd done in Dundee with that whole completely-missing-the-battle-because-he-slipped-in-pigeon-poo thing) there was someone around to pick up the pieces, sometimes literally. If he failed this time, though – if he'd typed in the wrong code or entered it too late – Arnold Armstrong's life would be forfeit and there'd be no one else around to save the day!

Murdo felt hollow and sick and stressed. He wanted to crawl into a darkened corner, curl up in a ball and go to sleep, and then wake up when everything was OK, and his mum would bake cookies and let him watch cartoons and he'd never have to worry about anything important ever again.

But his mum didn't arrive to comfort him and there wasn't a cookie in sight. Murdo stood before that maddening vault door, his heart sinking further and further with every passing second.

And then, just as all hope seemed lost, there was a slow whirring sound from some unseen cog turning nearby. On and on it spun, slowly, strenuously, until at last something clicked and pinged and the heavy vault door swung open! Murdo felt a great swell of warm, fuzzy happiness, like all of his birthdays had come at once. He yelled with delight and shot inside without a moment's hesitation.

It was dark in the vault. When Murdo's eyes adjusted, he saw a large display case containing the crown jewels, sparkling under a sprinkling of small spotlights. Murdo wasn't into old, museum-type stuff, but even he had to admit that the jewels looked pretty cool up close. There was the gem-encrusted Sword of State; the Sceptre, presented to King James IV by the Pope in 1494; and the Crown, made of Scottish gold and studded with glittering stones.

Each item was priceless, no doubt about it, but as far as Murdo was concerned they were a bunch of glorified accessories, a means to an end, bargaining chips to be exchanged in return for Arnold's safe release. As he made to smash the case, however, Murdo was struck by a nagging doubt that had been weighing on his mind ever since Longlegs had delivered his cruel ultimatum: how could he be sure the villain would actually release Arnold once he had what he wanted? He was a baddie, after all. A crook. And crooks are hardly the most trustworthy of souls.

"No," Murdo declared at last, after some careful consideration, "I won't simply hand these over. I'll hide them somewhere Longlegs will never find them, force him to release Arnold first, and then together we can defeat that lanky menace once and for all!"

Not a bad plan, to be fair. There's just one thing Murdo hadn't counted on: a gigantic robo-hand gliding silently into the vault while he was distracted, creeping up on him and then knocking him aside with a nonchalant flick of its wrist. Which is exactly what happened next. The fist then shattered the display case with a well-placed prod and scooped up the jewels.

When Murdo got back to his feet a few moments later, he was alone in the vault. The ground was littered with shards of glass and the crown jewels were gone.

"Great running raccoons! *Now* what am I supposed to do?"

There really wasn't any other option but to go after Longlegs and hope that he'd keep his side of the bargain, so Murdo burst into action. He didn't have time to navigate his way back through the cramped corridors and down those spiralling staircases, so he threw a chair at the first window he saw!

Funny thing about windows, though – they don't actually smash at the slightest thing like on TV.

Murdo persevered, battering the window with the chair again and again. Nothing. He stood there, panting, and then he was struck by a sudden moment of inspiration. He took hold of the window's shiny silver latch and pulled.

"Well, it's worth a try!" he reasoned. And would you believe it? The window swung open. "Sweet!"

Then he was outside, sliding down the castle walls, ready to take on the villain – ready for anything! Well, almost anything. But not so much for the sight that welcomed him in the courtyard below...

Daddy Longlegs was lying flat out, spreadeagled, his long limbs limp and lifeless. Above him stood Arnold Armstrong, free as a bird and seemingly unscathed, striking a typically heroic pose for the photographers and journalists who had magically materialised in time to capture the moment. Much to Murdo's relief, Arnold was also clutching the crown jewels, safe and sound!

It's over! And we've won! Murdo thought excitedly as he slipped off the wall and onto solid ground. Those deep, suffocating feelings of hopelessness he'd experienced in the palace were replaced by an overpowering sense of pure joy. Still, his mind couldn't quite absorb it. *I can't believe we won! I mean... how did that even happen?! Wait, no, that doesn't matter, Murdo, don't overthink this. Arnold's alive, Longlegs has been defeated and the crown jewels are out of harm's way! But if all of those things are as delightful and as wonderful as I think they are, then why on Earth is Arnold giving me the stink-eye?!*

Sure enough, as Murdo wandered across the court-yard, Arnold's eyes locked onto his with a glare so full of utter loathing and quiet fury it made him shake in his bright green boots.

"Um, hi," Murdo said tentatively.

"*Hi?* Don't you *hi* me, you little twerp!" Arnold snarled through gritted teeth, all the while maintaining an immaculate, beaming smile for the cameras.

"Sorry?"

"You will be sorry, you incompetent clown! I mean honestly, do you have *any* idea what you almost let happen? Centuries-old artefacts, handed over willy-nilly to this D-list, freak-of-the-week halfwit! Now smile, you ninny: we can't have the press finding out you almost lost the crown jewels – they'd have a complete and utter field day!"

Murdo was dumbfounded. "But... but he was going to, you know, squeeze you to death!"

"Um, *hello?* Do you even know who I am? I'm *invulnerable*, genius, as in 'totally impervious to harm'. I was never in any danger of being squeezed to death. Everyone knows that! Even Lanky Longlegs here knew that. He was obviously just hoping that you were as stupid as you look and that you'd fall for his bluff like the rank amateur that you very clearly are!"

"But I heard you screaming in pain when Longlegs tightened his grip on you..."

"I was yelling at you not to fall for his flimsy threats and laughable lies, you empty-headed fool!"

Despite the vicious beating Murdo had suffered that day, Arnold's words were by far the most painful thing he had ever experienced in his short life. They stung worse than a hundred bottles of TCP on a thousand freshly scraped knees, worse than stubbing every one of your toes and bashing your funny bone on the edge of a table covered in thorns, worse than landing in a pit of poisonous snakes while having your hair pulled by a ten-tonne gorilla and your teeth drilled by the dentist! To be put down so severely by his hero, by the man he'd idolised for years and modelled his whole existence on... It was torture, pure and simple.

Murdo bit his lip to keep it from trembling. There had to be something he could say or do to turn this around. "But you beat him... You escaped and saved the day, just like you always do, so it's all OK, right?"

"I got lucky. His arms and legs malfunctioned for some reason, just died on him out of the blue. If not for that..."

Murdo felt as though he was being sapped of what little energy he had left. His shoulders slumped and his head went down as he battled to hold back the tears.

Arnold noticed that the lad was taking this hard and his expression softened.

"Look, I appreciate that you were trying to help, but I don't think this whole 'superhero thing' is right for you. Maybe there's something else you could focus your energies on, something slightly less… heroic. You're just not made of the right stuff for this line of work. Now, take a few steps back so you're not in any of these pictures for the newspapers. Standing next to a scrawny bag of bones like you would probably make me look even more devastatingly handsome than ever, but I don't want anyone thinking I've got myself another useless teenage sidekick."

When Murdo boarded his return train late that afternoon, he was tired and sore and desperate to cuddle up in his bed… but he still tried to put a positive spin on his day.

He'd taken on his first real supervillain and had lived to tell the tale, plus it turned out his arm wasn't broken after all, which was a wee bonus.

He'd kind-of-almost had a team-up with one of Scotland's greatest superheroes, and not a lot of people can claim to have done that.

And once he'd finally got around to having lunch in the somewhat out-of-place castle courtyard tearoom, it was absolutely delicious.

Still, he couldn't stop thinking about what Arnold had said, and couldn't help but wonder if maybe his former role model was right. Perhaps he wasn't cut out for being a superhero after all…

EVIL RATING 💀💀

HEIGHT (CM) —
150 (WITHOUT STILTS)
1,200 (WITH STILTS)
INTELLIGENCE — 50

STRENGTH — 71
SPEED — 74
FIGHTING SKILLS — 40

BIO

Angus Arbuckle always had a bit of a bee in his bonnet about being short. As if being taunted at school wasn't bad enough, when he was older and started trying to get a good job, he often felt he was overlooked because of his diminutive stature.

Eventually becoming bitter and twisted, Angus started blaming everyone else for his misfortune and turned to a life of crime.

Believing that he was too short to be taken seriously, Angus took the name Daddy Longlegs and looked into ways he could boost not only his height, but his chances of becoming a successful super-criminal, too.

Originally Longlegs used a pair of wooden stilts to give him a height advantage over would-be adversaries, but he proved to be a bit of a pushover.

Next he tried an enormous inflatable costume, but that was a bit of a let-down.

Then he designed spring-loaded artificial leg extensions, but that idea was quickly bounced.

Finally he contacted a Japanese toy company and commissioned them to manufacture robotic arms and legs for him. And the rest, as they say, is history!

TRIVIA

Favourite word: Pumpernickel
(It's fun to say — try it!)

ARNOLD ARMSTRONG

HEIGHT (CM) — 185
INTELLIGENCE — 48
STRENGTH — 90
SPEED — 60

FIGHTING SKILLS — 50
SHOE SIZE — 7½
(BUT HE TELLS
PEOPLE HE'S A SIZE 9)

BIO

Arnold was once the world's most rubbish wrestler. He was slow and clumsy and a bit of a wimp. The guy couldn't wrestle his way out of, well, anything! Frustrated with his lack of success, he quit the pro-wrestling circuit and became a florist instead, because flower arranging had always come quite naturally to him (and he liked to make things pretty — but in a really macho way).

Then he volunteered to try out an experimental shampoo designed to make hair stronger, thicker and more healthy looking, but when he got it home the big idiot mistook the shampoo for a fruit smoothie and downed the whole bottle!

The one-of-a-kind formula made him super-strong, strengthening his muscles as well as his hair.

These days Arnold is still slow and clumsy, but he's completely impervious to harm and is generally considered to be the mightiest man on Earth. Plus, his hair is now stronger, thicker and much more healthy looking!

He still enjoys flower arranging in his spare time...

8.
READ ALL ABOUT IT!

Murdo emerged from his room the next morning filled with dread. Not at the prospect of having to do battle with an evil fiend, nor at the possibility of having to deal with his mum should she find out he'd lied to her about going to the zoo with his friends. No, Murdo was much more worried about what the newspapers might say regarding his epic fail in Edinburgh.

The thought of it had kept him up all night, front-page headlines spinning around in his mind...

His mum was watching the lunchtime news when Murdo shuffled awkwardly into the living room, still sore from the beating Daddy Longlegs had given him.

"...Chief of Police Scotland was keen to move attention away from the sharp increase in superhuman criminal activity and focus instead on the record number of superhuman arrests recorded over the past few weeks. He went on to suggest that the streets have in fact become significantly safer since the opening of **THE SLAMMER**, the new, multi-million-pound maximum-security prison that has been specially designed to detain superhuman criminals, and which so far boasts a flawless record with no reported breakouts. **THE SLAMMER**'s creator, Doctor Stor—"

"Stuff and nonsense," Murdo's mum said, switching off the TV. "There must be more important things to report on than a bunch of pretentious pansies prancing about in their pyjamas. I'd much rather see an in-depth investigation into how my son somehow manages to sleep in past breakfast and lunch every Sunday without fail. *That* sounds like a proper piece of hard-hitting journalism... don't you think, dear?" she smirked, glancing over her shoulder to where Murdo stood in his Adventure Squad pjs.

"Whatever you say, Mum," he replied. "Have you finished with today's newspaper?"

"Yes dear, I read it over breakfast – three hours ago!"

"Uh, cool. Thanks."

Murdo helped himself to a nutritious bowl of Captain Scotland Choco-Pops (they turn the milk tartan!) and took this morning's copy of *The Sunday Post* to his room. He could hardly bear to look at it. He closed his eyes and slowly unfolded the newspaper, forced one reluctant eye to edge open... and then let out a huge sigh of relief when he found that he hadn't made the front page.

The lead story was actually about the Adventure Squad foiling a mysterious supervillain called Chaos King, who had attempted to trap Celtic Park stadium in some kind of pocket dimension, along with the 60,000 fans who were there at the time. "Must be a Rangers supporter," Murdo decided. The picture that accompanied the article showed Greenfly Guy airlifting the defeated Chaos King out of the stadium, while Psychic Sally shook hands with the relieved Celtic boss. Murdo grinned stupidly as he remembered how Sally had leapt to his defence in Dundee. He gazed dreamily at her picture for a moment before returning to the task at hand.

Murdo figured his magnificent blunder at the castle would be featured somewhere, but pages two and three were given over to more coverage of the Chaos King event. Page four was all about the Flying Scotsman, a veteran superhero from Stornoway. He had saved a planeload of passengers from the nefarious Porridge Princess and her erstwhile husband Oatmeal Man (don't ask – the less said about those two the better). Then there were a few pages about boring stuff like politics and the economy before Murdo opened the centre spread: a feature article celebrating Captain Scotland's long and illustrious career.

As he continued flipping through the paper, Murdo grew more and more frustrated. His Edinburgh Castle catastrophe was nowhere to be seen, and his initial feeling of relief at not having his name dragged through the mud was soon replaced by one of sadness at not being mentioned at all. *There must be some kind of mistake. Yesterday was a big deal, wasn't it? How could it not be in the newspaper? Does the world really care so little for* SLUGBOY *that everyone would rather ignore what happened than so much as mention me??*

Then he saw it. Tucked away below a special report about family pets that look like Hollywood actors was the headline, **ARMSTRONG AVERTS JEWELS THEFT**. The picture showed Arnold standing triumphantly over Daddy Longlegs and, if you looked very closely, you could just see the end of Murdo's cape at the edge of the photo.

Murdo poured over the story, then spluttered furiously, spraying soggy Choco-Pops: "It doesn't say a thing about me! Not one single word. It's like I wasn't even there! This is ridiculous! This is outrageous! This is... this is... I'm too furious to finish my angry outburst!"

Murdo didn't finish his Choco-Pops, either. He set his bowl aside and pulled a large, leather-bound scrapbook out from under his bed. Inside the book were cuttings from newspapers and magazines: stories and articles featuring all of Murdo's favourite heroes.

Flicking through the scrapbook, he was struck by the number of recent stories he'd saved. In the last three weeks alone he'd filled up two-dozen pages, which was more than he'd used during the whole of the previous year.

That report on the TV was right, Murdo thought. *There has been more superhuman activity lately – a lot more! This could be important! Maybe I should contact the Adventure Squad on their twenty-four-hour helpline, or post a message on Captain Scotland's Twitter account, or maybe... maybe... Ach, who am I kidding? If an amateur like me only just noticed this today, the proper superheroes will have been on top of it for weeks. It's probably nothing, anyway...*

OMINOUS INTERLUDE

OH NO...

At around about the same time, not so far away, a solitary figure sat in a large, grand chair at the top of a long table in a dimly lit room, absent-mindedly cracking his fingers while he watched the lunchtime news.

"...since the opening of **THE SLAMMER**, the new, multi-million-pound maximum-security prison that has been specially designed to detain superhuman criminals, and which so far boasts a flawless record with no reported breakouts..."

There was a hesitant knock on the door and in came a sheepish-looking henchman. "Pardon the interruption, sir. More of your, uh... *guests* are arriving."

The shadowy figure at the table didn't turn. He simply said, "See them to their quarters," and gave a half-hearted wave of his hand.

"Yes, sir, uh... I'll get straight on that, sir," the henchman mumbled, awkwardly bowing his head and edging out of the room.

Alone once more, the dark figure afforded himself a dark smile in his dark room, as dark thoughts swirled around his dark head. All he needed now was a dark cat on his dark lap to complete the look. And a scar! He didn't have one, but he thought that'd look pretty sweet too.

"Everything is proceeding exactly as I had planned," he rasped, an evil glint in his eye, and then he flicked onto another TV channel, sat back in his large, grand chair, and dug into some toffee popcorn while watching 'Mighty Mutant Monkeys from Mars'...

END OF
OMINOUS INTERLUDE

9.
WE'RE ALL SOGGY GOING ON A SUMMER HOLIDAY

Brilliant rolling hills of green, strewn with the glorious purple hues of wild heather swaying gently in the breeze. Sunshine shimmering on the water's surface like a thousand tiny diamonds. Skies of pure blue; air fresh and crisp. *That's* the Loch Ness you see on postcards. *That's* the Loch Ness Murdo and his mum were expecting when they set out on their annual summer caravan trip. But sadly that's *not* the Loch Ness they found when they arrived...

Every summer, Murdo and his mum – let's call her 'The Big M'– spent a week on holiday in their caravan somewhere in Scotland, because The Big M doesn't like to fly. "Besides," she always said in a floaty voice, as if auditioning for a role in Visit Scotland's next TV advertising campaign, "Scotland has so many natural wonders, why would you possibly want to go anywhere else?"

In previous years they had gone to Glencoe and the Cairngorms and journeyed to some of the islands like Skye and Harris. This year they were staying at a caravan park near Loch Ness.

Even though it meant being stuck – trapped! – in a confined space with his mum for a whole week, Murdo was actually looking forward to getting away for a while. After last week's not-so-successful trip to Edinburgh, not to mention his embarrassing pigeon-poo episode in Dundee, he needed something to take his mind off superheroics for a little while.

The Big M had planned for them to do lots of boring stuff while they were away, like going shopping and visiting galleries, but she'd promised kayaking, mountain biking and a visit to Urquhart Castle too, so Murdo had agreed not to moan too much. Plus, to kick off their holiday in style, The Big M had booked a cruise around Loch Ness itself on their very own private-hire boat. Yeah, that's right: Murdo and his mum were going Nessie-hunting!

It could have been amazing. It *should* have been amazing. Unfortunately it started off anything but amazing. You'll recall the rolling hills and blue skies I mentioned earlier? Yeah, you can forget about those. And as for the gently swaying purple heather, the crisp air and the shimmering water... Don't make me laugh! No, when Murdo and The Big M found their way to the cruise pick-up point, the air was about as crisp as a soggy hanky. A thick fog billowed, enveloping everything for miles around and bringing with it a light but persistent drizzle, the type that soaks you, slowly but surely, chilling you to the bone. And the rickety old pier where they were waiting for their boat looked less sturdy than a blindfolded ostrich carrying a plate of jelly along a tightrope!

Somehow, though, The Big M remained remarkably chirpy. "Ah, the great outdoors," she sighed happily. "Makes you happy to be alive, doesn't it?

Murdo tried to look keen for his mum's sake, glancing occasionally at his watch as the minutes ticked slowly by. The boat was running late. It should have been there fifteen sodden minutes ago and before the cringe-worthy Mum-clichés started up.

"Good things come to those who wait," The Big M proclaimed brightly.

Murdo groaned and tried to change the subject. "Mum, do you really think superheroes are a bunch of pretending pansies?" he asked, recalling what she had said the other day when she'd been watching that news report about the new supervillain prison, **THE SLAMMER**.

"*Pretentious* pansies, dear, and yes, I do. I can't for the life of me think what could possess any rational young man or woman to dress up in one of those gaudy outfits and start taking the law into their own hands. I blame the parents."

Ha! If only you knew.

Another ten minutes passed by. Just as Murdo was about to suggest that perhaps the tour had been cancelled, a low, booming rumble broke the silence: a horn!

"Finally!" Murdo cheered. "This Nessie-hunt is going to be incredible! It's going to be mind-blowing! It's going to be... Oh! Um... that's not quite what I was picturing in my head..."

An old, feeble-looking craft limped into view through the fog. Murdo could just about make out its name, *Pier Pressure*, barely legible through rust and chipped paint. He crossed his fingers and hoped that the quality of the cruise was better than the quality of the pun...

A short, stocky man greeted them as they stepped gingerly onto the creaking boat. "The name's Sparrow," he said, gnashing on a battered old pipe and blinking his one good eye. "Captain Jock Sparrow. It's a pleasure to make your acquaintance this fine day." Captain Jock sported a bushy white beard and spoke like a cartoon character.

Sadly, the tour of the loch was woeful. Everything was just... grey. Occasionally there was a large, slightly darker grey patch, which might have been a hill, or a whale, or a low-flying hot-air balloon, or a whale flying over a hill in a hot-air balloon, but Murdo couldn't be sure. Nessie himself could have sailed past in a neon pink battleship and Murdo would have been none the wiser.

Although the water was reasonably calm, the boat still rocked to and fro, which made Murdo's tummy squish and squeeze. Not a nice feeling. He walked to the back of the boat and peered over the edge, expecting to see his own queasy-looking reflection on the surface of the murky water, staring back at him. What he saw instead were two large red eyes glaring at him from below the surface.

It was probably too much to hope that it was just a really big, angry fish...

10.
A BIG MESS
IN LOCH NESS

Ever had one of those days when nothing seems to go your way? Lately, Murdo had been having a lot of days like that, and today was shaping up to be no exception. The weather was awful. He was standing on a floating scrapheap. And there was a mean-looking pair of burning red eyes scowling at him from under the water.

"Um, Captain Jock? Are there any, like, sharks or octopuses in the loch?"

"It's not unheard of to come across a bigger-than-average brown trout, lad, but that's about as big and scary as they come round these parts. Why do you ask?"

As if in response to the captain's question, a dozen long dark tentacles shot out of the water, surrounding the boat on every side – port, starboard and, uh, those other two sides I don't know the names for. They coiled themselves around the vessel, bringing it to a sudden, shuddering stop. Murdo automatically made to press his belly button and transform into **SLUGBOY**, but a shrill shriek halted him mid-press. One of the mysterious tentacles had wrapped itself around his mum's waist and was trying to drag her overboard!

It's remarkable how many different things can go through your mind in an instant. Case in point: faced with the prospect of seeing The Big M yanked off the boat into the gloomy loch by a terrifying tentacle, three options presented themselves to Murdo:

Option 1: Become **SLUGBOY** and rescue The Big M. That seemed the most obvious course of action. But Murdo's mum didn't know he was a superhero – no one did – and he didn't want her or Captain Jock revealing his dual identity to the world (it's a superhero thing).

Option 2: Run over as plain old Murdo McLeod and try to help The Big M that way. He wouldn't be able to slide up surfaces or generate slime without transforming into his alter ego, but then maybe that wouldn't make much difference against those terrible tentacles anyway...

Option 3: Charge below deck, find Captain Jock's harpoon gun and lay into those tentacles the old-fashioned way, hacking and slashing at them until his mum was free. Sadly, that third option hinged on Captain Jock actually owning a harpoon gun, and somehow that didn't seem likely.

So yeah, all of that went through Murdo's mind in the space of about three or four seconds, by which point it didn't actually matter what he decided because...

The Big M had already gone ahead and freed herself! She'd slipped off one of her shoes, a seven-inch-heeled beast that made lesser shoes tremble with fear, and had driven said heel firmly and repeatedly into the tentacle that grasped her around the waist, puncturing it with deep, oozing wounds until it released her and scrambled away.

"Wow," Murdo said, suitably impressed. "Way to go, Mum!"

That was one problem solved then, but it wasn't long before another, much bigger problem reared its ugly head. Like, literally.

The red-eyed creature rose from the depths like an immense black shadow, a gigantic, brutish behemoth that dwarfed Captain Jock's increasingly shaky little craft. But this was no Nessie. It wasn't a mythical beast, nor some sort of prehistoric creature. This was a machine: an ancient-looking thing made of blackened steel, bronze and rubber, covered in seaweed, with oily pistons and valves, gears and pulleys, like some elaborate steampunk nightmare come to life.

Flames flickered behind its blood-red eyes, a furnace blazing in its metallic skull. The machine wasn't humanoid – it didn't have arms or legs in the traditional sense. Instead masses of thick rubber tentacles protruded from its misshapen metallic body, whipping and lashing with enough destructive power to turn *Pier Pressure* into little more than kindling and scrap metal.

Murdo looked on in awe as the machine wrapped more tentacles around the boat.

This is awesome, he thought, *but in a really scary we're-all-going-to-die way.* He dodged a tentacle as it tried to whip itself around his ankle and ducked below another that swung for his head. Murdo found he was able to avoid them so long as he didn't stand still for any length of time. The Big M and Captain Jock were doing a bang-up job of keeping the coils at bay, too. Murdo's mum swung her handbag viciously and stabbed with her high heel, while Captain Jock punched and kicked, grabbed and pulled, pushed, bit, chopped, jabbed, stamped... you name it, he did it! He was like a little terrier!

"You're not so tough," Jock called. "Think you can roll up to my beautiful boat and start making trouble, eh? Think you can throw your weight about, do you? You're nothing but a juiced-up, oversized children's toy!"

The machine responded with a series of grating metal sounds, scraping, groaning, grinding, before another set of tentacles – slimmer, faster ones – shot out from either side of its head. Avoiding these was much harder. In the confusion, Murdo lost sight of The Big M.

"Mum? Where are you?" he called. He lost focus for only a fraction of a second, but that was long enough. A skinny tentacle gripped his arm, jerked him to the ground with a painful bump, and then dragged him towards the edge of the boat. He tried desperately to grab onto something, anything that would keep him from being pulled overboard, but the tentacle hauled him this way and that before he could get a grip.

This is it, Murdo thought, scrambling franticly. *This is the end. Maybe it's just my time. Maybe everything happens for a reason. Maybe I'm as bad as Mum when it comes to rattling off tired clichés —*

Then suddenly The Big M was there, stabbing and slashing with (wait for it...)

...a harpoon gun! She attacked with surprising ferocity, taking only moments to free her son.

"Wow, Mum, where did you get that harpoon gun from?" Murdo asked, shaking off the last remnants of the sliced-up tentacle.

"What, this little thing? I found it in the captain's quarters. I didn't think he'd mind me borrowing it." The Big M seemed to be getting cooler and cooler with every passing emergency. Who knew she had it in her?

So far Murdo and The Big M had somehow survived the tentacle attack with nary a scratch to show for it, but the same couldn't be said for their boat. The deck started to splinter and snap below their feet as the tentacled machine applied more pressure.

"We need to get out of here," The Big M said. "Where's the captain?"

Murdo scanned their surroundings until he caught sight of the diminutive seadog. Jock was in the machine's clutches, his arms pinned to his sides, his legs kicking furiously. Then he was tossed into the loch like a filthy old rag being chucked in the bin.

Murdo raced over to a rubber life-ring, skipping and ducking and weaving to avoid being snared by tentacles. He threw the life-ring towards the splashing captain. Alas, Murdo wasn't the best judge of distance, so instead of landing just shy of Captain Jock, the life-ring battered the side of the little man's head.

"Ow!"

"Oops! Sorry, Cap!"

Then Murdo's mum was calling from behind him: "Murdo, look out!" She shoved him in the back, knocking him off his feet, just before a big tentacle crashed down between them, smashing the boat down the middle, leaving Murdo on one side of the gaping hole and his mum on the other!

Then, quick as a flash, a half dozen tentacles wound around The Big M's wrists and ankles, disarming her of her handbag and shoe and hoisting her into the air.

"Murdo, get out of here!" she shouted. "Get to safety!"

Yeah right, as if he was really going to abandon her. She could be a real pain in the butt sometimes, but she was the only mum he had! Besides, she'd saved him twice today already – it was about time he returned the favour! *If only she'd pass out,* Murdo thought, *then I could press my belly button and slide into action!*

But could he really afford to wait for his mum to faint before leaping to her rescue? How much did it really matter if she found out he was Slugboy? It's not like she would sell the story to the newspapers... *But what if she bans me from being a superhero?* He could see her now: "Why not get a more sensible, less dangerous job, dear? I'm sure there are lots of things you could turn your hand to with your particular set of skills. What about the world's most wonderful window cleaner? You wouldn't even need a ladder!"

Murdo shivered at the thought of it.

But no matter what the future held, he had to do something – before it was too late!

11.
FAST
AND FURIOUS

It was now or never. If Murdo was going to save his mum, he had to act – and quickly – or risk losing her forever. Before he'd had a chance to even move, though, in the blink of an eye, The Big M was back on her side of the boat, tentacle-free and none the worse for wear.

"Great galloping greyhounds! What just happened?" a mystified Murdo asked no one in particular.

"That would be me," replied an American-sounding voice, and then a boy appeared before Murdo, completely out of the blue. He was a skinny lad in a padded jumpsuit fitted with knee-pads, elbow-pads and wraparound sunglasses, grinning under an untidy mop of spiky blonde hair. Murdo immediately recognised

MAXIMUM VELOCITY

– the quickest kid alive!

Before Murdo had a chance to speak, Max was off again. "Wait! Where are you..." A somewhat soggy Captain Jock materialised, as if by magic, at The Big M's side. "...going?"

"Sorry about that." Max skidded to a halt next to Murdo. "Thought I'd better save the old-timer, too. Where were we?"

"I think you were about to say hello."

"Huh! That *does* sound like something I'd do!" Max grabbed Murdo's hand and started shaking it so fast it made his teeth chatter. It was like holding onto a pneumatic drill! "Hi! Hello! How are you? You're good? Great! Me too! Beautiful weather we're having, huh? Nice day for a boat trip. Shame about the company! This robo-squid thing giving you trouble? Leave it to me! Oh, by the way, when did Pluto stop being a planet?"

"Wait, why do you..." Max disappeared again before Murdo could finish his sentence. "Man, I *wish* he'd stop doing that!"

The machine began focusing all of its efforts on flattening Max, probably perceiving the new arrival to be the biggest threat to its wellbeing, but the speedster evaded its swiping tentacles with ease, all the while blethering on about this, that, the next thing... and the next thing after that too!

"I mean, it *used* to be a planet and then – *BAM!* – it wasn't. How did that happen, and did anyone stop to ask the Plutonians how *they* feel about it? Man, this boat looks awful! Hope it's well insured! Or do you say 'ensured'? What's the difference between those two anyway? And whose idea was it to have two words with different meanings that sound almost exactly the same? That's insane!"

"Seems to be a lot of insanity going around..." Murdo grumbled under his breath as he watched Max zoom from one end of the smashed boat to the other.

Great plumes of smoke and steam poured out of the vent stacks lined up along the machine's head, like rows of enormous chimneys. It seemed to be growing increasingly frustrated at not being able to ensnare its target. Perhaps figuring that Max wouldn't be able to move so fast without something solid beneath his feet, the motorised monster battered the deck of *Pier Pressure*, utterly annihilating the vessel. But Max moved at such high speeds he was able to zip across the surface of the water like a speedboat. He raced this way and that, laughing at the machine and teasing it. The tentacles tried to catch him but only succeeded in getting tangled.

With the boat now smashed to smithereens, Murdo, his mum and a visibly upset Captain Jock were all floating about on separate pieces of wreckage, bobbing up and down like rubber ducks in a bathtub.

As Murdo tried to paddle his bit of broken boat

towards The Big M, Max hopped merrily onto a nearby barrel, keen to continue their conversation while the machine was occupied with its knotted tentacles.

"Methinks that machine got out the wrong side of bed this morning," he said cheerfully. "Man, that'd be some size of bed. Unless it sleeps in a giant hammock... but I digress! So, you were saying something about, err... You were saying something to do with... um, sorry, what were you saying again?"

"I was actually wondering why you keep prattling on about random rubbish and asking completely arbitrary questions while we're slap-bang in the middle of a life-or-death situation!" Murdo grumped.

"Ooh, 'arbitrary'– good word! And to answer your question, my good man, my mind works even faster than my feet, so it's constantly buzzing with a million and one thoughts and ideas! Makes it difficult to focus on any one thing for longer than a few seconds, I'm afraid, but I think I'm getting better at it! Did you know the word 'arbitrary' is derived from the Latin word *arbiter*, meaning 'supreme ruler'?"

"Fun fact," Murdo said, rolling his eyes. He hadn't meant this to sound quite so spiteful, but he was most definitely *not* a Maximum Velocity fan.

Max was relatively new on the superhero scene, but he'd already shown himself to be brash and cocky, and he didn't seem to take anything particularly seriously – a typical American superhero! What irritated Murdo most, though, was that Max wasn't much older than he was and had only been on a couple of notable adventures, but was already building a faithful following among diehard superhero fans on both sides of the Atlantic. Meanwhile Murdo was still languishing at the bottom of the great superhero heap... and that was totally unfair!

Still, Max *had* saved The Big M and Captain Jock from a watery end; the least Murdo could do was be polite.

"So what are you doing in Scot—" Murdo started, only to be cut off once again.

"Hold up. Check it out." Max pointed towards their copper-plated opponent.

With its tentacles currently out of commission, the robotic monstrosity switched tactics, unveiling two huge turbines at its centre covered in massive metallic spikes. They looked like the world's most enormous, most frightening set of razor-sharp teeth. The turbines started to spin in sync, pulling in water and sea life and fragments of boat – and annihilating them. Murdo was closest to the machine, and he was getting closer with every passing second...

"Looks like you're in need of some saving, dude!" Max mused.

"Get my mum and the captain to shore first," Murdo told him. "I'll be OK. I'm a superhero, like you."

Max looked Murdo up and down quizzically. "Seriously?"

"Yes! Not every superhero is flashy and American and bursting out of their impractical spandex costumes with gigantic, rippling muscles you know!"

"Chill dude! I believe you! OK, I'll be right back! Don't go anywhere!" And just like that, Max was gone... and then he was back again. "P.S. Does your mum know you're a superhero?"

"Um, no..."

"Cool. I'll tell her I dropped you off on the other side of the loch so she doesn't worry!" And then away he whizzed. Within seconds, Murdo's mum had disappeared from her patch of wreckage. Jock was next. Max was so fast it was like they were vanishing into thin air. If Murdo hadn't known better, he would've sworn Max's power was teleportation.

"Show-off..."

With his mum out of danger and out of sight, Murdo was free to jab his forefinger firmly into his belly button: once again he became the sensational SLUGBOY! As his pint-sized piece of wreckage was pulled towards turbine-churning oblivion, however, it dawned on him that being in costume wouldn't actually make the slightest bit of difference to his predicament.

"Huh. It's possible that I didn't think this plan all the way through..."

12.
ROBOT
WARS

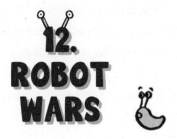

The machine's colossal turbines roared like a hungry monster as they spun faster and faster, drawing in debris and gobbling it up mercilessly. And it looked like Murdo was next on the menu! He strained to come up with some sort of ingenious escape plan as he was pulled towards what would likely be an extremely painful (not to mention messy) death scene, but instead of keeping a cool head under pressure or laughing in the face of danger like superheroes are supposed to do, Murdo panicked and begged for mercy. But, you know, in a really manly way.

"Don't eat me don't eat me don't eat me!" he screamed, relieved no one could see him.

"Cool costume," Max beamed, perching precariously on the edge of some wreckage. Murdo hadn't even noticed him returning. He eyed the speedster suspiciously, not sure if this costume comment was sincere or an attempt at taking the mick.

Probably the latter, Murdo decided. *What a jerk.* "How long have you been sitting there?"

"Long enough," Max grinned. "Do you need a hand?" he offered, as they careered ever closer to the certain doom of the thrashing turbine teeth.

Rather than ask that big-headed blow-hard for help, Murdo made a desperate leap from his little bit of boat to another smashed section of *Pier Pressure*. He landed a split second before his first bit of boat was destroyed by the machine's horrific spinning appendages. Then he hopped, skipped and jumped from one floating piece to another until, finally, the machine's mighty turbines ground to a halt.

Max stood on top of one of the turbines, clutching the end of a disconnected power cable. "Guess I pulled the plug on that attack, huh?" He laughed.

Murdo panted, relieved and exhausted, but the metal monster wasn't done yet. It howled at the boys, infuriated at being thwarted. Steam gushed from its vent stacks. Metal strained and groaned as it finally yanked its tangled tentacles free of each other and started slashing wildly at its prey. Murdo ducked, yelping as tentacles whooshed past – three measly millimetres from his face! – leaping about awkwardly to avoid being turned into chop suey. Meanwhile, out of the corner of his eye, he saw Max feinting to the left, darting to his right, dodging with such ease and grace Murdo felt a tinge of jealousy.

The machine's fortified feelers flayed furiously at Max, but its attacks were proving ineffective. Murdo balanced unsteadily on the remains of what looked like a ship's door. "I don't suppose you have a plan?" he asked.

"That depends," Max replied, "do you have any powers that might be useful, like invulnerability, increased agility, telekinesis, plasma blasts or the uncanny ability to explode giant robots with your mind?"

"Um... no. I slide up walls and, err, I can make slime."

"Ah. In that case, I need you to wait right over... here!"

Murdo suddenly found himself standing on solid ground, surrounded by grass and trees, looking out over the misty loch.

"What just happened?" he asked, feeling slightly disorientated.

Max was standing next to him. "I happened," he said. "I carried you here at super-speed. It was probably too fast for your brain to process. I need you to stay here until I've taken care of that tin-plated terror."

"Wait, you want me to sit this one out like some kind of... defenceless bystander?"

"No, dude, I want you to stay here and act as a second line of defence," Max told him. "You're no use to me out there on the water, but if I can't stop that thing, if it somehow makes it past me, then at least I know you're here, ready to protect the innocents and foil the fiend!"

"Oh! Well, when you put it like that... I suppose that *does* sound pretty important. Don't worry, Maximum Velocity, you can count on me!"

As usual, Max was long gone before Murdo reached

the end of his sentence, but for once he wasn't bothered – not now that he had a job to do!

Murdo struck a commanding pose and waited, on guard and ready for action.

Ten minutes later Murdo was still waiting – and he was getting really bored. "I'm pretty sure superhero adventures are meant to be more exciting than this," he moaned, flipping another pebble into the loch.

He knew it was wrong, but the more Murdo thought about it the more he sort of secretly wanted Max to fail in his mission. *Then I could defeat the machine instead,* he mused. *Then it would be my name in lights, not his. I would be the one to get all the glory and...* "Great dancing dolphins! Max doesn't want me here to act as his second line of defence. He wants me to wait here so *he* can hog all the glory! That lousy good-for-nothing weasel – he's stealing my big moment! And to think I almost fell for it! Well he can forget about that!"

Without a boat and with no other means of transport, Murdo decided there was nothing for it but to swim to the rescue, so he immediately charged into the icy cold loch.

"Stupid, crummy, American superhero," Murdo spluttered as he splashed about in the dark water. "Coming over here, muscling in on all of my arch-nemesssis...

arch-nemissesis... on all of my bad guys! Just wait till I get my hands on him!"

But as time ticked on Murdo started freaking out. His imagination got the better of him.

What if Max's plan *had* backfired? What if he'd been hurt, or worse? What if he'd been killed... and people thought it was somehow Slugboy's fault for leaving him to fight that thing alone? Murdo pictured Aqua Lass and Arnold Armstrong laughing at the news that Slugboy had messed up yet again. "No!" he shouted. "That won't happen – I won't let it! I refuse to be the world's worst superhero!"

Murdo swam harder and faster, until at long last he burst through a bank of mist to find...

(short pause for dramatic effect)

...that everything was strangely calm.

The robotic behemoth floated limp and lifeless, its tentacles inert and drifting aimlessly. The scene was like a freeze-frame, like someone had hit a giant pause button and brought the machine to an abrupt stop, mid-attack. Bits and pieces of *Pier Pressure* bobbed gently on the surface of the water, but otherwise all was still and deathly silent. And Max was nowhere to be seen.

"He did it," Murdo gasped, half amazed, half bitterly disappointed. "He actually beat that thing... and robbed me of my chance to finally prove myself. But where is he?"

He's so fast, Murdo thought, *he's probably on the other side of the world by now, bragging about how wonderful he is and telling people how gullible I am. Man, just wait until people hear about this. I'll be a laughing stock! I might as well shred my tights now...*

"What's up, doc?" called a voice from above, snapping Murdo out of his train of thought. At first the voice seemed to come from the machine, which would have been weird, but upon closer inspection Murdo spotted Max standing on the machine's shoulder, next to its head, smiling and waving.

"Max! You're alive! You're still here! You're... opening up a hatch on the machine's shoulder and climbing inside...?"

"Yep, I'm going in. Taking the plunge. Venturing into the unknown. Going where no man has gone before!" Max stopped for a moment to flick some slimy seaweed off his shoulder. "Care to join me?"

"But wait, what happened?" Murdo couldn't keep the confusion out of his voice. "How did you stop the machine? How do you know you're not walking into a trap? And how is it your hair doesn't get totally windswept from all that high-speed running you do?"

"Dude, chill out! Live a little! And leave the arbitrary questions to me! Come on, I'll explain everything inside," Max said, and then he disappeared into the small, round hatch.

"Stop! Shouldn't we wait for a proper grown-up superhero to arrive?" Murdo asked, but Max was already gone.

Murdo slid up the side of machine. He reached the hatch and peered inside. A ladder led down into a dark tunnel and out of sight. Murdo had a really bad feeling about this, but he couldn't just walk away now – not if he wanted to prove once and for all that he was a proper superhero.

With a lump in his throat (and a serious case of the heebie-jeebies), Murdo made his way down the ladder into the dark dank tummy of the tin terror...

13.
INTO THE
DEPTHS

The air got hotter and stuffier the further Murdo descended the long rusty ladder, which seemed to go on forever. He couldn't see anything of his coal-black surroundings, but he could hear Max chattering excitedly further down the thin passageway and was struck by a stale fishy smell that made his tummy churn.

Finally he splash-landed into mucky ankle-deep water, where Max was waiting.

"This is brilliant!" the speedster gushed, holding his nose. "Who knew there were so many fun things to see and do and *smell* in Scotland?"

The boys found themselves in a narrow tube-like tunnel with rounded walls and a low ceiling. Sporadic strip-lights were spread out along the sides of the tunnel, disappearing around bends in either direction. Something about this place made Murdo uncomfortable and kind of queasy. It wasn't the heat or the stench. It wasn't the company, either (although that wasn't exactly helping his mood). There was something... *off* about this place. Murdo couldn't quite put it into words, but it made him feel that he and Max shouldn't be there.

Whatever it was, Max didn't seem to share Murdo's unease; he simply picked a direction and cheerfully led the way with a spring in his step.

"So what's your name? Your superhero name I mean," Max asked.

"I'm **SLUGBOY**," Murdo said proudly.

"Ha! Good one! Well, sort of. Actually no, I don't get it, but never mind. What are you really called?"

"I'm called Slugboy," Murdo said. "That's my name."

"Seriously?"

"Yes! Why is that so difficult for people to believe? I have slug powers and I'm a boy. What else would I be called?"

"Mollusc Man! Sergeant Slime! Super Slug!" Max replied enthusiastically before realising that it was a rhetorical question.

Wading through the tunnels was like trawling through sewers. Murdo's face felt greasy and his costume stuck to his sweaty arms and legs. He had to hold the end of his cape to keep it from dragging through the filth. There were flies buzzing around, and twice now Murdo had felt something cold and scaly slithering by his feet. Both times he'd taken it completely in his stride:

"AAARGH!"

"Really?" Max asked. "Again with the screaming?"

Sorry, did I say he took it in his stride? What I meant to say was that he screamed like a wimpy kid hurtling uncontrollably along the world's scariest rollercoaster ride while being poked and prodded by goblins and pecked repeatedly by ravenous zombie blackbirds.

Both times.

"It's probably just an eel or a barracuda or something," Max said. "Ooh, or a coral reef snake! Highly venomous, those ones..."

"That's not exactly comforting." Murdo's mood was growing darker by the minute. It didn't help that Max kept yammering on about how exciting this was, and reminiscing about other adventures he'd been on, occasionally breaking off from those stories to share useless trivia about American football and music, or asking random questions about Scotland.

It didn't take long for Murdo to get over the gratitude he'd been feeling to Max for saving The Big M's life earlier. Soon all he could think about was how annoying the guy was and about how every word out of his smug mouth seemed to grate.

"Want some gum?" Max offered, after listing every American Super Bowl winner since the turn of the century.

"No, I don't want any of your stinking gum, you motor-mouthed loser! I hope you choke on it – at top speed!" That's what Murdo *felt* like saying. What he *actually* said was, "Um, no thanks."

"Suit yourself. Speaking of suits, you can stick to walls, right? Couldn't you slide along the roof or the side of the tunnel to keep your costume from getting soaked in all this disgusting sewage?"

"Huh. Err... no, because... I'm conserving my strength! You know, in case we meet some baddies in here and I need to, like, defeat them in mortal combat," Murdo lied, because

a) he was too stubborn and embarrassed to admit that the idea hadn't actually occurred to him; and

b) he didn't want to give Max the satisfaction of knowing he'd had a really good idea.

Not that Murdo was petty or anything, but... Well, maybe he was a *bit* petty.

The further the boys went, the narrower the tunnels became. Murdo was beginning to feel suffocated. He tried to take short, shallow breaths to keep from gagging, but the stink was giving him a sore head and making him woozy. He wasn't sure how much more of this he could take. Desperate for a distraction from their grim surroundings, he asked Max how he'd defeated the machine. Please understand that this was a last resort. Listening to the speedster brag about his mighty victory was not Murdo's idea of fun, but if it took his mind off the sinking feeling in his tummy then it might be worth it. As it happened, Max was only too happy to describe every tiny detail of the titanic tussle.

"The Loch Ness Monstrosity is steam-powered, like an old-fashioned train. Steam-powered machines need fire to heat the water in their boilers, which create steam, and the steam makes everything else in the machine work. Of course fire needs oxygen in order to burn, so I figured that the stacks along the top of the Loch Ness Monstrosity must be where the oxygen gets in. All I needed to do was block them somehow and hope that the robotic rust-bucket would run out of steam – pun very much intended, dude!

"There was plenty of debris floating about from your dear departed boat, so that was a good start. It took a few runs – I had to speed up and down the side of the machine a couple of dozen times, avoiding being grabbed by those pesky tentacles – but eventually I got those vent stacks stuffed full with junk. Then I took moss and some other bits and pieces from around the shore and crammed them into every gap and hole in the big tin can of a machine. Then I raced around it again and again until the water in the loch started churning and swirling."

"You made a whirlpool?" Murdo asked.

"Nah, I made a maelstrom, which is like a whirlpool, only stronger. It's normally caused by the meeting of conflicting currents, but in this case running around in circles at top speed created the same effect."

"How do you know so much about whirlpools and 'mail-storms' or whatever?"

"What, you guys don't get the Discovery Channel over here? Anyway, the maelstrom kept the Monstrosity from attacking me, and by way of a happy coincidence I also accidentally caused a vortex effect, like a tornado, that sucked out what little air the machine had left inside of it, thereby extinguishing its flames and leaving it powerless. Ta-da!"

Murdo didn't like to admit that he was impressed... so he didn't (even though he was). There was just one detail nagging him: "You keep calling this machine the 'Loch Ness Monstrosity.'"

"Indeed I do, my friend."

"Do you actually know what this robo-octopus thing is, then?"

"Oh sure," Max replied. "I mean, I've read about it in magazines and history books. I can read at superhuman speed, so I've read pretty much everything there is to read on superhero history."

"I read too, you know!" Murdo said defensively.

Max didn't seem to take offence. "I don't doubt it for a microsecond, bud. Not for a nanosecond, a femtosecond, not even for a yoctosecond! So you've heard of the Monstrosity, too?"

"Uh, no..."

"Not to worry, dude, that's probably because it's so ancient! It's like a total relic, made in the dim-and-distant past by

MAJOR DISASTER

when he was really young and inexperienced, right near the beginning of his supervillain career. On a slightly unrelated note, did you know The Beatles hold the record for the most number one singles in the US, but in the UK it's Elvis who's had the most? You'd think it'd be the other way around, but no!'"

Murdo stopped dead in his tracks. "Wait. What?"

"I know, it came as quite a shock to me, too, but it's completely true from tip to toe. The Beatles had twenty US chart-toppers, compared to eighteen for Elvis."

"No, I didn't mean... Errrgh! Not that! What you said before! Did you say... Did MAJOR DISASTER make this floating fortress?"

"He did."

"*The* Major Disaster?"

"The one and only."

"But he's the most notorious, most deadly villain of all time."

"Uh huh, yep, he sure is!"

"He's the guy who single-handedly overthrew the US government and held the entire Northern Hemisphere to ransom; the guy who tried to freeze the sun and extinguish all life on Earth – for a dare; the reason the original Adventure Squad formed, because the only way they could defeat him was by working together and combining their talents."

"Uh, yeah, dude, I know. Everyone knows that."

"And *he* made this thing?"

"Yes."

"And we're inside it, working our way through a labyrinth of tunnels, with no idea where they lead or what we might find when we come to the end of them?"

"That's about the gist of it."

Murdo glared at Max. "Are you crazy?! We can't be here! We have to get out – *now*! I mean, what if he's actually here? Great deep-sea-diving dodos! We could be willingly marching towards a slow painful death at the hands of the most fearsome, most reviled rogue in history!"

"Dude, seriously, chill out! Take a few deep breaths, OK? Major Disaster hasn't been seen or heard from in years! The chances of him actually being here are, like, a million to one."

"But what if he actually *is* here?"

Max grinned, a mischievous little twinkle in his eye. "Well, we're not going to find out by standing around here chatting, are we? Come on!"

As Max merrily darted around the next bend and out of sight, Murdo found himself wishing he'd stayed in bed that morning...

14.
THE BELLY
OF THE BEAST

After slogging through the tunnels for what seemed like hours (it was ten minutes...), Murdo and Max came to a set of metal steps leading out of the revolting water and up to a resilient-looking vault door with a small electronic keypad. ("Why did it have to be another vault door?" Murdo grumbled.)

Max tried turning the five-pronged spindle-wheel door handle, but it wouldn't budge. "It's locked."

"Aw, that's too bad, we can't get in without the pass code," Murdo said, trying to sound disappointed, but secretly overjoyed that they couldn't go any further. Meeting Major Disaster, the most despicable villain of all time, wasn't high on his to-do list (being wiped off the face of the planet by said villain wasn't high on his list, either). "Oh well, we tried! I guess we should be getting back to—"

"Not a problem, my friend!" Max smiled as he went to work on the keypad, his fingers becoming a blur as they whizzed over the digits. This continued for all of seven seconds, and then the keypad bleeped.

A tinny voice said, "Welcome, Master," and the door hissed open like an enormous hungry-sounding snake.

"Aw man, how did you do that?" Murdo asked.

"There were nine digits on the keypad, plus zero," Max explained casually. "I assumed it would be a four-digit password, meaning there could only be around ten thousand possible combinations. I just worked my way through them until I got lucky, starting from quadruple zero."

"Oh, that easy, huh?" Murdo muttered quietly to himself. "Stupid, lousy, poor-man's-excuse for a super-hero... *Ooh, everybody look at me, I can open doors, I'm so special...*"

"What was that, sorry?"

"Huh? Who, me? I didn't say anything!"

The boys entered a vast room full of computer equipment and tools, beakers and flasks, TV screens and microscopes, and dozens of other things that Murdo didn't recognise.

"Where are we?" he asked.

"Dude," Max gasped, "I think this is Major Disaster's laboratory! His inner sanctum! The beating heart of his evil empire! This is... so totally awesome!" He looked like he was about to burst with excitement. "I'm going to check things out, search for signs of life or, you know, evil people. You stay here and keep watch. And don't touch anything until I get back – just in case!"

Max zoomed off, kicking up clouds of dust in his

wake, leaving Murdo free to explore and touch things and not keep watch.

"*Don't touch anything*," he imitated in a sing-song American accent. "Whatever, *dude*. Who died and made you the boss of everything?"

The lab was stuffed full of inventions and experiments, most of which seemed unfinished. There were shelves of test tubes filled with green and purple and luminous blue liquids; large glass jars with bizarre body bits floating in them; incomplete suits of hi-tech armour. Murdo even found a freeze ray mounted on the wall (because every supervillain needs a freeze ray). Sadly, he couldn't get it to work – not that he wanted to use it on Max to shut him up or anything...

Venturing further into the darkest recesses of the lab, Murdo was disturbed and disgusted by what he found: a whole section of the workshop had been dedicated to experiments on animals, with some seriously messed-up results. Peculiar creatures occupied hefty vats: an exotic bird with razor-tipped wings, body armour and the tentacles of a baby octopus; an enormous rat with sharp, metallic teeth and a laser canon fused to its back; a chicken with the head of a fish – or was it a fish with the body of a chicken? Either way, they were some of the strangest and most unsettling sights Murdo had ever seen.

Beyond these there were trolleys laden with bizarre instruments, shelves full of textbooks on physics and chemistry, magnetism and dark matter, string theory and genetic engineering, and most excitingly of all, tucked away in the furthest, darkest corner of the lab, propped precariously on a small, silver stool, Murdo stumbled across... a huge pile of vintage comics!

He approached the pile cautiously. 'Don't touch anything,' Max had said.

Murdo hesitated, but then he saw which issue was sitting on top of the pile:

"*Implausible Bulk*, issue 180," he whispered breathlessly, rubbing his hands together greedily, hardly believing his eyes. "One of the rarest, most valuable comics in existence, featuring the first appearance of Skunk Bear, my all-time favourite fictional superhero! I know it'd be wrong to just take it, but there's no one around and... and I just can't help myself. I have to have it! I have to have *my precious*—"

He reached for the comic, only to have his hand slapped away painfully.

"What are you doing?" said Max. "Are you as nutty as a fruitcake? A few sandwiches short of a picnic? As batty as a... uh, bat? Those comics could be booby-trapped!"

"Oh. Uh, yeah, I knew that. Just keeping you on your toes, you know?"

"You were? Of course you were!" Max grinned. "For a split-second there I thought you were a complete idiot, or totally insane, or so incredibly naive as to believe that you could just go around helping yourself to some of Major Disaster's most prized possessions without setting off some sort of apocalyptic self-destruct device that would surely obliterate us and everything else within a twenty-mile radius! Silly me!"

"Silly you!" Murdo laughed nervously, before swiftly changing the subject. "So, any sign of you-know-who?"

"Lord Voldemort?"

"Err, no, Major Disaster."

"Oh! No, there's no one here besides us and some prehistoric robot security guards."

"What?! Security guards?! Where?!" Murdo choked, looking from side to side.

"Oh, don't worry about it, they're defunct. I think their batteries ran out. Nothing seems to be working down here – not even the freeze ray."

"Bummer."

"I know, right? I've always wanted a freeze ray. You know, because they're so cool. Get it? *Cool?* See what I did there?"

"Um, yeah, wow... real funny..."

The boys wandered back through the laboratory. In the centre of the room was a large, square table covered in blueprints and schematics, maps, diagrams, spreadsheets, graphs and a half-eaten Mars bar.

"Dude, check this out!" Max held up a well-used, leather-bound journal. "It's like an instruction manual on how to combine electronic engineering with biological organisms, and it's written by Major Disaster himself!"

"Electric engineering and bio-what now?"

"Living things, dude, like plants and animals and, you know, people."

"So Disaster has been splicing together living things and machines, like that rat with the laser and the bird with the razor-tipped wings... but why?"

"To enhance them, bro, make them faster and stronger and more deadly."

"But what's the point in that? What would he want a bunch of all-new, all-deadly souped-up super-pets for?"

"Maybe he was planning on making an army of these things to help him take over the world or something."

"So what stopped him?" asked Murdo. "It's like he just abandoned this place right in the middle of all these experiments."

"Who knows? After his last prison break a few years ago, he just completely disappeared. People thought maybe he'd had enough and packed it in, retired to some exotic paradise island, or rocketed into space to colonise another planet."

"But then how did the Loch Ness Monstrosity get activated?"

"Search me, dude. Doesn't look like there's been

anyone here in years. I guess someone could have started it up by remote control..."

"Someone like Major Disaster?" Murdo gulped.

"It's possible..."

Murdo didn't like the sound of that. Suddenly he wanted to be as far away from the Loch Ness Monstrosity as a person could be. Luckily he had the mother of all excuses up his sleeve. Literally. "Look, my mum's probably worried sick about me. I should head back. Can you call the Adventure Squad and let them know what we've found?"

"Yeah, dude, totally. I'll pop in and see them on my way home."

"Thanks. Oh, and thanks for saving my mum earlier, too. She's a bit of a nightmare sometimes, but she means well. At least, I think she does... Most of the time."

"Don't mention it; it's what I do! And hey, nice team-up, huh? We should do it again sometime! See you soon, dude! Keep it real!"

In an instant, Max was gone and Murdo was alone in the lab, with no intention of hanging around! But as he made for the exit, he couldn't shake the feeling that he was being watched. He looked around one last time before he slipped out through the vault door, but didn't see the blinking red lights of the security cameras that had been monitoring his every move since he entered the Loch Ness Monstrosity...

ANOTHER OMINOUS INTERLUDE

"There's another new arrival checking in, sir, the third in as many days. Calls himself:

The Iron Emperor of Unspeakable Suffering.

Charming fellow. All he was interested in was finding out when breakfast is served... Um... Are you listening, sir?"

The henchman cleared his throat as loudly as he dared, but the dark figure sitting at the top of the long table didn't budge. He was glaring intently at his TV, cracking his fingers and chewing on Highland Toffee. The screen displayed a black-and-white image of two costumed boys.

The henchman edged further into the dark room. "Something the matter, sir?"

"This is security footage from aboard the Loch Ness Monstrosity," the dark figure explained. "The taller one is called Maximum Velocity, a superhero from the States."

"And the other one – the small, awkward-looking lad with skinny arms and legs – who's he?"

"I haven't got a clue." The dark figure shrugged.

"Frankly, I don't care. He looks about as dangerous as a Tunnock's Teacake. But the speedster could prove problematic. Get me everything you can on that one, just in case."

"Yes sir, right away sir!" the henchman said. He marched out as quickly as possible, leaving the dark figure alone in his dark room, with his brand new dark cat resting sleepily on his dark lap.

"I've come too far to have my plans ruined by the likes of you," the mysterious villain rasped, poking the screen and scowling. Then he sat back in his big comfy chair and finished his toffee while reading the latest issue of *Implausible Bulk*.

But who is this enigmatic evildoer, you ask? What is his diabolical scheme? And why is he always sitting in the dark? The answers to all of these questions and more will become clear SoOOOOOOoon...

END OF
OMINOUS INTERLUDE

EVIL GENIUS WEEKLY

MAJOR DISASTER

EVIL RATING 💀💀💀💀💀

HEIGHT (CM) —
 TOO SCARED TO ASK
INTELLIGENCE —
 OFF THE SCALE
STRENGTH — STRONG ENOUGH

SPEED — FASTER THAN YOU
FIGHTING SKILLS —
 UNKNOWN — AND I WOULDN'T
 WANT TO FIND OUT!

BIO

Little is known about Major Disaster's origins, but his exploits are the stuff of legend, so let's focus on a couple of his more audacious bids for world domination.

KNOWN WEAKNESSES

Major Disaster has a pretty severe peanut allergy and suffers from hay fever during the summer months (not quite the same as kryptonite, is it?).

There was the time he hijacked all the TV satellites and threatened to broadcast nothing but badly dubbed Mexican soap operas until the world's most powerful nations decreed him The King of Everything. Fortunately, Disaster's feeble-minded minions got their wires crossed, so everyone was treated to re-runs of classic 'Mighty Mutant Monkeys from Mars' episodes until Glasgow-based superheroes **The Astonishing Saltires** were able to reclaim the satellites.

Later in his career, Disaster tried to wipe out all of Earth's technology using a sophisticated, self-aware computer virus, but the virus worked a little too well: upon activation, it immediately identified itself as one of the world's most advanced technological developments, so self-destructed before eradicating anything else. Whoops!

Major Disaster relies on an array of hired goons, gadgets and evil allies to do his dirty work, which is often where his plans fall down. His current whereabouts are unknown; some believe he's dead, others think he's merely biding his time before making an out-of-this-world, over-the-top, phantasmagorical comeback. Only time will tell...

AWESOME RATING *POW* *POW* *POW*

<u>HEIGHT</u> (CM) — 170
<u>INTELLIGENCE</u> — 75
<u>STRENGTH</u> — 50
<u>SPEED</u> — 95

<u>FIGHTING SKILLS</u> — 40
<u>ATTENTION SPAN</u> — ERR,
LET'S JUST SAY 'LIMITED'
AND LEAVE IT AT THAT

BIO

Maximum Velocity (real name: Maximus Rapido) is the son of Prince Nimble of the Supersonic Speedballs, an extra-terrestrial race of hyper-accelerated speedsters who live their lives in fast-forward. His mother, however, is human, so Max was raised on Earth and now serves as ambassador to the throne of Lickety-Split, his father's home planet.

Though relatively inexperienced, Max more than makes up for that with foolhardy impulsiveness and a complete disregard for safety, two characteristics that have made him exceedingly popular with teenagers everywhere.

Fun fact: Every week Max goes through approximately 14 pairs of trainers, 28 pairs of socks and 1 whole can of Sure For Men antiperspirant.

TRIVIA

Moving at high speeds is Max's natural state, so he's capable of maintaining his optimum pace for extended periods of time. However, it takes a considerable amount of effort and concentration for him to slow down. He actually finds restricting himself to human speed much more tiring than zipping across continents at his regular breakneck velocity!

15.
HOME IS WHERE THE  IS

Murdo's back was against the wall. He was cornered, with no means of escape. He'd tried everything, but his adversary was as brilliant as she was relentless and she simply couldn't be stopped. This, it seemed, was the end of the line for Slugboy! But it wasn't some mad scientist or a killer robot he was facing. Not a rogue alien, nor an evil mutant. No, this was something far more deadly than any of those threats. This time Murdo was going toe-to-toe with... his mum!

"Are you ever going to tidy your room? Sit up straight! What time do you call this? Don't sit so close to the TV! I suppose you expect that plate will somehow magically clean itself, do you? It wouldn't kill you to help out around the house every once in a while!"

Having seen his mum in a new light recently, when they'd bravely battled the Loch Ness Monstrosity side-by-side, Murdo had thought that maybe the two of them might start afresh when they arrived back home. Maybe they'd have a new-found respect for each other. Maybe she'd become more laidback after her near-death experience: a happier, more pleasant person to be around.

Well, that flight of fancy had gone straight out of the window last night at dinner.

"Don't speak with your mouth full! Don't chew with your mouth open! Chew up your food before you swallow it! Ask if you may be excused before leaving the table! No, you may not be excused from the table, how rude! Finish your vegetables!"

At times like these Murdo thought his mum would make a fairly formidable supervillain: the catastrophic *Colonel Cliché*, able to produce predictable, overused phrases at the speed of twenty mums! Or maybe she'd be called *Mrs Nags-a-Lot*, Scotland's moaniest mum.

Normally when she launched into one of her signature rants, Murdo didn't offer much in the way of resistance. He'd learned the hard way that it was often easier to just give in to her demands. This afternoon, however, Murdo's mum had crossed the line...

"Nope, no way, not happening!"

"I'd go myself, but there's so much washing and ironing to do, and I need to dust and hoover and change the sheets on the beds, clean out the cupboards, cut the grass... and I was going to make soup!"

"What kind of soup?"

"It's a new recipe I found online. It's very nutritious."

"What kind of soup, Mum?"

"Spinach with anchovies."

"Ugh! What did I do to deserve that?"

"Oh, come on, Murdo!"

"No!" Murdo protested vehemently.

You see, his mum had asked him to pop down the High Street to pick up a few 'essentials' from the pharmacy for her. And by 'essentials' I mean a basketful of products specifically designed to embarrass you when you take them to the till, e.g. anti-fungal foot powder, anti-lice shampoo, coconut body butter and a bumper pack of triple-quilted, super-sensitive, aloe-vera loo roll for delicate bottoms. That would have been bad enough as it was, but Callum Campbell's big sister worked at the pharmacy. She was a world-class gossip and she absolutely *hated* Murdo. If she spotted him buying body butter and super-sensitive loo roll, everyone in St Andrews would know about it in the time it takes you to get to the end of this sentence. Anyway, that's why Murdo was dead set against it.

But then his mum unleashed her secret weapon: a finely honed guilt-trip.

"Is it really so much to ask when I work my poor fingers to the bone to provide for you, to clothe you and feed you and to pay for all those ridiculous comics you read? Not to mention those nine long months I carried you—"

"Whoa! Stop! Enough already! I'll go! I'll go!"

"Aw, that's my special boy." Murdo's mum beamed, pinching his cheek.

Man alive, Murdo thought, *my mum's an evil genius!*

Despite being the height of summer, it was a very windy day in St Andrews (it's always windy in St Andrews). On his way to the town centre, Murdo struggled to suppress a wee giggle at a couple of passing tourists huddling together for warmth. The large, moustached man wore three-quarter-length khaki shorts, a Hawaiian shirt and an expensive-looking pair of sunglasses. He had his nose buried in an unwieldy folding map of the town, strutting along with no regard for the people in his way, coming up for air very occasionally to take a few snaps on a big obnoxious camera. The petite woman clinging to his arm looked completely frozen. She was dressed in a sleeveless leopard-print dress and was too engrossed in her telephone conversation to pay even the slightest bit of attention to what was going on around her.

Soon Murdo was on Market Street, but instead of going into the pharmacy as per his instructions, he sauntered past it and entered the bookshop a few doors down.

The last few weeks had been a trying time for Murdo. Sure, he'd met the Adventure Squad and Arnold Armstrong – that was cool – but most of his adventures had ended in failure. His battle with the Loch Ness Monstrosity hadn't been so bad, but it'd been quite stressful having his mum in the firing line – and playing second fiddle to Maximum Velocity hadn't been much fun, either. All in all, Murdo was feeling a bit frazzled.

At times like this, when he was in need of a wee pick-me-up, Murdo enjoyed nothing more than flicking through some comics. Reading about his favourite superheroes, seeing them foil ostentatious evil-doers with nary a hair out of place... it gave him hope that, one day, he might be just as brilliant as they were.

Murdo had decided that rather than come into the bookshop with a pack of loo roll the size of Mount Kilimanjaro tucked under his arm, he'd check out some comics first and then nip into the pharmacy on his way home. After all, his mum hadn't specified a time by which he needed to get back, so he didn't suppose there was any rush. It seemed a fairly foolproof plan, but then things don't often go smoothly when Murdo's involved...

Twenty minutes later, Murdo was nestled comfortably among the book stacks, eagerly leafing through the latest edition of *Samurai Stick Insects*. Woodlouse Woman and Beetle Boy were trapped, and Lieutenant Ladybird had just unleashed the Army Ants of Doom, and they were all about to be involved in a massive, all-out, no-holds-barred super-insect brawl when suddenly—

"AAAARGH!"

Murdo heard screams and shouting coming from outside.

Through the large front windows of the shop, he could see people on the street standing stock-still, mouths gaping, eyes wide in disbelief, while others ran past, terrified. Those tourists from earlier were milling about, too. The man in the Hawaiian shirt was still occupied with his map. The woman in the leopard-print dress was still yakking away on her phone. Both of them were utterly oblivious to the chaos unfolding around them.

While the other customers huddled at the windows to see what all the fuss was about, Murdo sneaked behind the Julia Donaldson display near the back of the shop and pressed his belly button. In a flash he was dashing to the door, calling in his deepest, most manly voice: "Never fear, citizens! No matter the danger, SLUGBOY shall Thor it!"

"I think you mean 'thwart'," the girl behind the counter offered helpfully.

"You might be right!" Murdo cried, bumbling out onto the street. "Never did think that made much sense, now that you mention it."

A frantic crowd charged down the road like a herd of stampeding buffaloes. Panic-stricken people slammed into one another, knocking each other over, trampling those who couldn't keep up. Murdo had to slide up a wall in double time to keep from being squashed.

"Don't be alarmed," he shouted, but it was a rather half-hearted effort at reassurance, as he was beginning to feel somewhat alarmed himself.

When trying to take control of a difficult situation, it's important to exude authority, to have a commanding presence and to give clear, concise instructions in a calm, steady voice. I'm sorry to say that our Murdo had no presence whatsoever – most people hadn't even noticed he was there – and he blurted vague, flustered instructions like, "OK, so, let's move, people. Quickly now, but take your time! Hurry up! Don't rush!" Public speaker of the year he isn't! Not that the great Scottish public were helping matters. Suffice to say, Scots don't take too kindly to being ordered around by a skinny little kid in tights.

"Take a hike, squirt!"

"Outta my face, shrimp!"

"Mind your own business, peewee!"

Realising that he wasn't having quite the impact he'd hoped for, Murdo gave up on crowd control and slid further up the wall to get a better view of whatever it was everyone was running from.

Then he wished he hadn't.

Towards the end of the street, Murdo could see something big and hairy going berserk, howling and throwing its weight about, leaving two neat lines of overturned cars in its wake. He immediately recognised the beast from its distinctive red, blue and green fur: it was the

 ,

a ferocious savage brute the size of an elephant, remarkably strong and renowned for his intolerable cruelty. And suddenly Murdo had an overwhelming urge to flee along with the crowd...

16.
SLUGBOY VS. THE
TARTAN TERROR

OK Murdo, think! What are the Tartan Terror's weaknesses? He doesn't like reality TV shows, but then who does? Um... With all that fur he must be highly flammable, but setting the guy on fire wouldn't be very heroic of me... Oh, I've got it! He reverts back to human form if he goes too long without drinking Irn Bru, so all I need to do is keep him from taking a swig of the fizzy orange stuff for a little while and he'll become completely harmless within... um... Actually I have no idea how long that might take, but a flimsy plan's better than no plan at all!

The shops along Market Street in St Andrews are terraced – meaning there aren't spaces between the buildings – so Murdo was able to slide along the shop fronts towards the creature without having to leap from one wall to the next. That was the good news. The bad news was that he was no match for the Terror, so keeping him busy, even for a short space of time, could prove somewhat difficult.

And by 'difficult', I mean 'fatal'.

The Terror is incredibly strong and resilient, Murdo thought as he slid along the shop fronts, *but he's slow, too. If I keep a safe distance from his furry clutches I should be OK. But how do I keep him occupied until his Irn Bru wears off?*

Good question.

Then Murdo saw what the Terror was wearing on his head and realised his plan was toast, burned before it had even begun. The fuzzy fiend was sporting a hard hat with Irn Bru cans clumsily taped to either side of it. Two pink curly straws led from the cans straight into the monster's mighty mouth.

"Give me a break!" Murdo moaned. "So much for keeping him off the Irn Bru..."

He looked back down the street towards the fleeing crowd. Most people were far enough away now to be out of danger, but there were still one or two stragglers.

Right, Plan B it is. Just keep him busy until everyone gets to safety. Distract him somehow. Simple!

Yes, unbelievably simple, Murdo, much in the same way that spelling 'conscientiousness' is simple, or that counting every hair on your head is simple...

Pop quiz, folks! Which of the following options do you think would be the most effective method for catching the attention of a rampaging monster?

a) Offer to buy him a cheeseburger and then have a heart-to-heart with him about his feelings.

b) Dazzle him with an array of breathtaking party tricks, such as juggling while riding a unicycle, or burping the alphabet backwards.

c) Shout at him and call him names.

Murdo opted for shouting at him and calling him names. I would've picked the second option myself, but I'm just the narrator, what do I know?

"Hey, fuzz features! Up here, you overgrown hairball!" Murdo called from high on the front wall of Starbucks. The Terror took no notice, focusing instead on bending lampposts into shapes like he was making balloon animals (now *that's* a party trick!).

"Oh, so you're just going to ignore me, huh? Try ignoring *this*, you woolly weirdo!" Murdo shouted as, in a moment of madness, he threw himself off the wall and onto the awning of the clothes shop next door. He bounced on the awning, using it like a trampoline to propel himself through the air towards the Tartan Terror. For a heart-stopping moment it looked like Murdo was going to fly clear over the top of his target and land in a heap, but luckily he managed to stretch out an arm and grab hold of the monster's fur.

Landing on the Terror was lovely. No really, it was! It was like throwing yourself onto the world's biggest fluffiest duvet. Sadly Murdo couldn't afford to get too comfortable – he had a job to do. He punched the Terror right in the back of his giant fuzzy head, below the hard hat, but his fist sunk harmlessly into the great wad of fluff as if he'd punched an enormous ball of cotton wool.

The Tartan Terror marched on, not noticing Murdo at all.

"Oh, so I'm not worthy of your time, eh? Well, how about *now*, huh?" Murdo karate-chopped his foe. "Or why not try on one of these for size? Take THAT! And THIS! And two of THESE!" Murdo punched, kicked and tugged for all he was worth, but the Terror didn't bat an eyelid.

Well, at least he hasn't eaten me, Murdo shrugged, looking on the bright side as usual. Then he saw that the crowd at the end of the thoroughfare seemed to have stopped running away. In fact, a few people were coming back in his direction, towards the Tartan Terror.

What on Earth....?

Soon more people were streaming back towards them. Others spilled into the middle of the road from side streets, or poured out of shops they'd sheltered in. *But why?* Murdo didn't have to wonder for long.

Behind the crowd of terrified tourists and nervous natives came dozens of diminutive... *things*. Murdo wasn't sure how to describe them.

The pint-sized horrors were a strange mix of woodland animals and small household pets – rats, hamsters, hedgehogs, squirrels and guinea pigs – only they weren't cute cuddly bundles of love: these little beasties were miniature war machines. We're talking ferrets with metal jaws full of sharp silver teeth, and bunnies with laser-guided missile launchers mounted to their backs. Bizarre though these things were, Murdo couldn't shake the feeling that he'd seen them somewhere before...

More and more of the furry fiends were climbing down from rooftops, crawling out of drains and scuttling closer from either end of the road. As they set about blocking all of the escape routes, the Tartan Terror slowed his pace. There was no need for him to rush – these people pouring into the street weren't going anywhere. His stomach growled as he loomed ever closer, licking his lips.

The crowd started freaking out and Murdo, still getting the world's weirdest piggyback ride on the Terror's shaggy shoulders, wasn't coping much better.

This is a nightmare, he thought. *This is even more of a nightmare than having to buy Mum's embarrassing stuff from the pharmacy! I figured maybe, if I was lucky, I could slow the Terror down long enough for everyone to get away, but they're stuck here now... And as for these robotic rodents, sure, I can probably squash a whole bunch of them, but there are hundreds! Face it, Murdo, you're in way over your head, as usual.*

Murdo was in such a flap that he didn't notice the sudden buzz of the crowd until a pale elderly gent thrust a bony finger skywards and croaked, "Someone's coming!" The old man waved his arms and stamped his feet like an excited child when he saw who it was, battering his walking stick excitedly on the pavement. The crowd sounded a chorus of elation – and Murdo had to pick his jaw up off the ground – as someone descended from the heavens like a hardy-looking angel in a kilt, with a plaid cape billowing majestically in his wake.

The sounds of cheering and whooping filled the street as the incomparable

the people's champion and the country's premier superhero, arrived to save the day!

17.
THE GOOD,
THE BAD AND
THE ~~UGLY~~
FUZZY

The Captain Scotland.

The guy was superhero royalty, an absolute legend, and there he was, hovering unsteadily in mid-air next to Carphone Warehouse, munching on a bacon and egg sandwich, wearing his vintage 1925 Scotland rugby shirt inside-out and back to front. Murdo was so caught up, staring at him like some sort of starstruck groupie, he momentarily forgot he was perched on top of the fuming furball otherwise known as the Tartan Terror.

"What's this hubbub about then, eh?" Captain Scotland mumbled through a mouthful of bacon and egg, spraying sandwich everywhere and knocking over a bin as he landed.

"This overgrown flea-bitten hairball is attacking St Andrews, Cap!" Murdo shouted. Unfortunately for him, the Terror didn't take too kindly to being called flea-bitten. He reached up and snatched Murdo by the cape, plucking our hapless hero off his shoulder like a monkey picking a nit, then flung him at Captain Scotland!

"Catch me, Cap!" Murdo called as he sailed past the good Captain, who was mucking about on his mobile phone.

"Huh?" Cap looked up in time to see Murdo crash-landing in a fruit and veg stall. "Sorry mate, I was trying to answer a call on this infernal thingamabob, but I can't seem to work the blasted thing. So, what's this hubbub about then?"

"You asked that already," Murdo replied, wiping squashed banana out of his hair. "Also, you have some egg in your beard."

"Maybe I do, but you're completely covered in fruit, my friend, so you're in no position to be lecturing me on personal hygiene! Now, where were we?"

"You need to stop the Tartan Terror before he makes shish kebab out of those people." Murdo pointed to the crowd being hemmed in by robotic rodents.

"Then that's what I'll do!" Captain Scotland decreed, before turning his attention to the crowd. "Good people of Glasgow!" he boomed.

"St Andrews," Murdo coughed.

"Good people of St Andrews!" Cap continued, "I'm going to go teach that great muckle beastie over there some manners, while my wee pal here – him in the red and blue pyjamas – cuts a path through those pesky little critters for you. Then if you'd all kindly walk in an orderly fashion to, err... someplace safe... that'd be marvellous." Captain Scotland turned to Murdo. "Think you can handle that, laddie?"

"Uh, I guess so."

Captain Scotland raised a wobbly eyebrow.

"I mean... Of course! You can count on me, Cap!" Murdo said.

"Braw! And as for you, you bloated mothball," Cap said, eyeballing the Tartan Terror, "prepare yourself for the hiding of a lifetime!"

Murdo watched in wonderment as Captain Scotland raced along the rooftops towards his ruthless rival without a hint of hesitation. He was so confident, so decisive in everything he did. Even when he stumbled off course and crashed into a chimney – "The bleeding thing came out of nowhere!" – he somehow made that look cool and heroic, too.

The mere sight of the Tartan Terror would be enough to turn most men into quivering wrecks, but Cap threw himself at the beast wholeheartedly.

"What a guy," Murdo said dreamily, before yelps from the crowd snapped his focus back to the task at hand.

Most of the crowd had been corralled around the large memorial fountain that stood proudly in the middle of the wide cobbled road. They were completely surrounded. People screamed as tiny metal jaws nipped at their heels. A few folk had managed to break from the pack, but with dozens of mechanical minions pouring in from all sides they didn't have anywhere to go.

Two guys tried climbing drainpipes to escape, but a group of vicious cyborg mice scampered up the pipes and munched the screws that fixed them to the wall, sending the men crashing to the ground. A goth girl dressed all in black was knocked off her skateboard by a six-legged, two-headed squirrel-bot. A posh-looking lady golfer who had been tottering about on the roof of her car, clutching her precious golf clubs, was bowled over by a trio of rocket-propelled hedgehogs. And nearby, those tourists that keep popping up – Hawaiian-Shirt Man and Leopard-Print Woman – had somehow scaled lampposts on either side of the street. Hawaiian-Shirt Man had tucked away his map of St Andrews and was taking holiday snaps of the commotion, while Leopard-Print Woman continued her phone conversation, sharing jokes and laughing out loud while people were fighting for their lives just a few feet below.

Murdo had seen enough. "Incoming!" he shouted as he whooshed into action on the goth girl's skateboard, swinging one of the posh lady's golf clubs like a Jedi on a sugar rush. His surprise attack scattered the main pack of critters, allowing the locals some breathing space. The wee beasties were quick to close in on him, but Murdo kept them at bay, swiping his club in wide looping circles. He battered a bionic badger on his backswing and connected sweetly with that six-legged, two-headed squirrel-bot on his follow through, sending it sailing across the road and smashing through a café window.

"Oi, watch it, mate!" barked an angry-looking man from on top of a white van. "That's my coffee shop you're vandalising! You'll be paying for that, you little thug!"

"You must be joking!" Murdo replied. "I'm trying to save you!"

"Save yourself!" the man shouted. "I didn't ask for your help! I was doing just fine on my own, thank you very mu—

AAARRGH!"

That's the sound of the guy not quite finishing his sentence because he was being monkey-piled by a band of mutated chinchillas.

"Unbelievable," Murdo muttered, launching a super-hedgehog through the windscreen of an Audi TT. "You try to do the right thing and what thanks do you get? Ungrateful, no-good, lousy, spoiled— *OUCH!* "

Murdo's rant was curtailed by a bite to the bottom! Then a nip to his knee and a gnash to his knuckle! It seemed the techno-creatures had deduced that the skateboard-riding, golf club-swinging boy with the squashed banana in his hair posed more of a threat than anyone else, so they were now ganging up on him. They swirled around, attacking in waves from different directions to keep him off balance and disorientated. Murdo thrashed about with his golf club, but he was quickly overwhelmed.

"No way!" he shouted as he disappeared under the swell. "No way am I getting taken out by a bunch of Sylvanian Family rejects! That's just... embarrassing!" He pushed away tiny scratchy claws and kicked furiously at the beasties clinging to his legs, but there were too many of them. For every creature he shook off, another two or three took its place. Then a chicken with the head of a fish (or was it a fish with the body of a chicken?) was right up in his face, and Murdo suddenly remembered where he'd seen these things before. These were the animal cyborgs he and Maximum Velocity had found in the lab aboard the Loch Ness Monstrosity – the ones Major Disaster had created!

Sadly, it didn't seem as though Murdo would be sharing his realisation with anyone anytime soon, or possibly ever. He grew more tired with every passing moment. The critters were jabbing him, poking and prodding him, gouging him with their sharp teeth. Weak and completely swamped, it looked like this might be Slugboy's last stand...

But just as he was about to give up the fight and collapse under the weight of his attackers, he heard shouting and jeering from the crowd. It was faint at first, like it was coming from far away, but it quickly grew in intensity. Then Murdo was able to make out what people were saying:

"Leave him alone!" cried a woman.

"Eat this, monster munch!" yelled a gruff-sounding man.

"Go back to the little pet shop of horrors, you filthy, foul-smelling, mutated dung beetle!" squealed an extremely articulate little girl.

Suddenly two strong hands broke through the horde of tiny tyrants, grabbed Murdo by the scruff of his neck and pulled him to his feet. It was one of the guys who had hurled insults at Slugboy during his earlier attempt at crowd control.

"Look alive, peewee," the man grinned. "We're here to rescue you!"

Scenes of sheer mayhem were unfolding all around, but it was good mayhem! The people of St Andrews were standing up for themselves, fighting back against the legion of furry fiends. An elderly lady swung her bag of groceries like a medieval mace, battering a nightmarish green cat with large red eyes and leathery black wings; a tough-looking teen with a skinhead and a nose ring drop-kicked a massive rat, like a New Zealand All Black booting a rugby ball into touch; the goth kid had got her skateboard back and was using it as a club against a mob of mega-mice; a student squashed a bird-snake hybrid thing with his pile of library books.

All over the place, people were revolting against their would-be oppressors – and before long they had the upper hand. The last monsters fled and elation filled the street! People cheered and high-fived complete strangers, their allies in what would henceforth be known as the Battle of St Andrews. Sounds too good to be true, right?

That's when an enormous, blood-curdling roar froze everyone in their tracks.

Murdo wearily lifted his head to look down the road, and then wished he hadn't, because the Tartan Terror was storming towards them... and Captain Scotland was nowhere to be seen.

18. MONSTER MUNCH

Faced with a horde of hi-tech critters, the citizens of St Andrews had risen to the challenge admirably, overcoming the odds to emerge victorious. But flattening a few techno-rodents is one thing; taking on the Tartan Terror – an immense, merciless brute who can crush cars with his bare hands – well, that's a different prospect entirely.

"Run," Murdo muttered, his body aching after a battering from the robo-vermin. He somehow mustered the energy to shout. "RUN! Everyone get out of here – now!" And for the first time in his short superhero career, people actually listened.

Murdo was soon standing alone in the deserted street. He made his way towards the Terror, trying to look tough and confident despite the fact he was as pale as a sheet and shaking like a leaf. He would have confronted the monster, too (and yes, would probably have been eaten alive), if not for that darned pair of tourists! You remember the ones – Hawaiian-Shirt Man and Leopard-Print Woman.

Murdo came across them crouching behind an upturned Range Rover outside Bonkers Gift Shop, and despite all the amazing things he had seen over the last few weeks, he couldn't quite believe what he was seeing this time. Hawaiian-Shirt Man was snapping away at the scenes of destruction on his big obnoxious camera, showing no concern whatsoever for the gravity of the situation. Leopard-Print Woman, meanwhile, had finally finished her telephone conversation, but now seemed to be texting.

"You two have to get out of here," Murdo said, crouching down beside them, glancing nervously along the street at the Tartan Terror. The monster had been distracted momentarily by a tasty-looking BMW, but he'd be on them in seconds. "Go now, before he sees you. I'll keep him occupied."

Hawaiian-Shirt Man took a photograph of Murdo and then spoke in broken English with a thick accent, "You are in, how do you say, fancy dress, yes?"

"What? No! I'm SLUGBOY."

"I am not understanding what this means, to be 'Slugboy'. This is medical condition, yes? You visit hospital soon?"

Murdo sighed. Clearly those Slugboy business cards he'd invested in had been a waste of hard-earned pocket money.

He peeked over the man's shoulder. The Terror was lumbering towards them, chomping on some leftover

BMW. "You have to go!" Murdo grabbed Hawaiian-Shirt Man and tried to move him by force, but the tourist was a solid lump of a man and shrugged away his efforts easily.

"I am thinking you are being very rude now. I am finding this most offensive. I am visitor to this country. I expect warm welcome. Hospitality, yes? I am not wishing to be manhandled by foolish child in foolish costume..."

Murdo tried to stop him, to warn him that the Terror was almost upon them, but Hawaiian-Shirt Man carried on regardless, even as a dark fuzzy shadow loomed over him.

"Dude, seriously, the Tartan Terror is—"

"...looking like something a little cat coughs up, yes?"

"Actually, I was going to say he's right behind you." Hawaiian-Shirt Man turned to find himself nose-to-nose with the Terror. "And what do you think it is that you are looking at, hmm?" He prodded the great, hulking beast with one of his chubby digits. "You are thinking I am to be scared now, yes? Ha! I find more scary things than you cleaning out shower back home! What do you say to that, hmm?"

By way of reply, the monster opened his mouth and belched flames, much to Murdo's surprise.

What the...? Since when can the Tartan Terror breathe fire? A puzzle for another time, perhaps, as there were slightly more pressing matters at hand.

When the smoke cleared, all that was left of Hawaiian-Shirt Man were two flame-grilled stumps sticking out of his loafers, and that stupid camera had somehow survived, too.

Leopard-Print Woman looked up from her phone. "I have been updating Facebook status," she said. "It is possible I may have missed something, yes?"

"Get behind me!" Murdo told the woman, although he wasn't sure how that was going to help anyone. He wasn't exactly fireproof. And if the creature had any other new powers up his hairy sleeve, well, this was going to be over even quicker than Murdo had anticipated...

The Terror grinned, picking charred bits of BMW out of his teeth with the car's bumper. Murdo looked around frantically, hoping to find something – anything – he could use to defend himself. Then, in a moment of desperation (or inspiration, or insanity, or something else entirely), he dived for that big obnoxious camera, sizzling quietly next to Hawaiian-Shirt Man's smouldering shins.

The Tartan Terror lunged at his prey. Murdo thrust the camera in the monster's face and squeezed the exposure button and ...

FLASH! - FLASH! - FLASH!

The Tartan Terror stumbled back, startled and blinded by the bright light, giving Murdo time to grab Leopard-

Print Woman by the arm and make a mad dash for it. Running away from a fight didn't feel very heroic, but Murdo knew he was well out of his depth – he decided he was probably more a 'shallow end' type of superhero. Unfortunately his improvised flash-attack didn't dazzle his fuzzy foe for long. The monster pounded the ground with his huge hairy fists, cracking the tarmac and rocking Murdo off his feet.

"Keep running until you reach the beach," Murdo told Leopard-Print Woman as he strained to get back up. "And then... I don't know... swim for it!"

Then he dusted himself off, turned to the Terror, placed his hands defiantly upon his hips and said, "Would it be OK to take a quick timeout right now? It's just I *really* need to pee."

Murdo guessed from the Terror's blood-thirsty glower that his answer was probably no...

19.
A HAIRY ENDING

The Tartan Terror was so close now that Murdo could feel the heat coming off his fur and smell his stinky breath.

"Dude, you are in serious need of a tic tac," Murdo joked. The monster howled and barged him over.

"Ouch! So that's how you want to play this, huh? Fine! I didn't want it to come to this, but if you don't back off – and I mean right now! – then I'll be forced to use my secret weapon on you!"

The Terror paused for a moment... and then gave a deep, rumbling chuckle.

"I'm serious!" Murdo protested. "This is your last chance, pal! Walk away, real peaceful like, or I'll put you down – hard!"

The Terror called Murdo's bluff. He lunged forward with surprising speed, his mouth gaping, tongue lolling, ready to take a sizeable bite out of our rookie hero. Luckily Murdo hadn't been bluffing about that secret weapon – well, not completely bluffing, anyway. While he'd been threatening the Terror, he'd quietly collected a handful of horrible oily goo – that yucky stuff he generates from his skin. As the beast approached, Murdo hurled the ball of goo into the monster's mouth.

SPLAT!

He knew it wasn't going to stop the Terror completely, but it should at least slow him down for a few seconds.

It should have, but sadly it didn't.

The Terror recovered almost immediately – and he was now doubly furious! He grabbed Murdo and pinned him against the side of a lorry. The air around them heated up, fizzing and crackling with energy. Murdo heard the flame ignite at the back of the monster's throat.

This is it, he thought. *Here comes fiery death. I guess there are worse ways to go. He could've sat on me and squashed me to death under his huge hairy bum...*

Then just as the Terror was opening his great reeking mouth to unleash his lethal flame-throwing attack... a pick-up truck landed on him.

Captain Scotland staggered into view looking lost and dishevelled but otherwise none the worse for wear. Murdo had never been so glad to see somebody in his entire life.

"Wow, you saved my life!" Murdo gushed. "Thanks, Cap!"

"Ah, so you've heard of me! Good! Listen, you've not seen a huge hairy bloke come this way, have you? Looks a bit like an unfriendly Furby."

"Uh, yeah... You just dropped a truck on him."

"I did?"

Murdo pointed to the hairy feet sticking out from below the battered vehicle.

"Ha! I guess I must have. Well, that's a turn up for the books. *Ding dong! The witch is dead!*" Cap sang.

Unfortunately his celebrations were cut short, because you can never keep a good supervillain down for long...

The Terror heaved the truck into the air, tossed it aside and then was up once again, grappling with Captain Scotland in a battle of monumental proportions. The two superbeings went at it tooth and nail, matching each other blow for blow.

Cap is widely regarded as one of the planet's most powerful people, but the Terror was holding his own. He dodged and weaved to avoid Cap's earth-shattering blows, responding with thunderous strikes of his own and flame-breath attacks.

This isn't right, Murdo thought. *There's no way the Terror should be holding his own against Cap. They simply aren't in the same league. Sure, Cap's getting on a bit so maybe he isn't in the best shape of his life, but the Terror's never been this fast and strong before. And the new thing with the fire...*

This is like Brodie Brainwave and Daddy Longlegs all over again. Those two villains were far more formidable than they should have been. What if this is all somehow connected?

And with the recent increase in supervillain activity they mentioned in that news report the other week, it's almost as if —

"Jings, crivens, help ma boab, man! This is my favourite kilt, you great bushy bampot!" Cap boomed, clutching loose bits of torn plaid material flapping in the wind.

The Terror spat out shredded tartan and snorted.

"You asked for this, you insufferable woolly mammoth!" Cap snarled.

Murdo clapped his hands excitedly. This could mean only one thing!

The sky grew dark and stormy as Cap's red beard became a fiery mane, his nose flattened, his face grew longer and his teeth sharpened to fine points. Lighting flashed as his torso stretched and rippled with fury, while his fingers and toes turned into enormous paws with dagger-sharp claws. The sound of distant thunder and Cap's mighty roar signalled that his transformation into the Rampant Lion was complete!

"I am *so* joining the CAPTAIN SCOTLAND fan club," Murdo whispered.

Cap made short work of the Terror after that; there aren't many who can compete with the mighty Rampant Lion. Still, Murdo was slightly surprised at how little opposition the Terror offered in the end. It was almost like he had stopped trying. Murdo wondered whether the fire-breathing had taken a lot out of the monster.

With the villain defeated and securely bound using Cap's magic sporran chain, people gradually returned to the scene and set about trying to put right the damage.

Captain Scotland, once again in his human form, took Murdo aside for a quiet word. Murdo hoped that maybe Cap would congratulate him for keeping the Terror busy when he had lost track of him, or say well done for helping everyone (almost everyone) get away safely. Based on the previous 'pep talks' he'd had from Aqua Lass and Arnold Armstrong, however, his expectations weren't too high. As it turned out, that was probably just as well...

"Look laddie... sorry, what was your name again?"

"My name's SLUGBOY."

"Oh. Well, not to worry, sunshine, names aren't everything. Anyway, today you did... OK."

"You really think so?" Murdo asked, perking up.

"Well, that one fatality aside, aye. Thing is, son, in this line of work 'OK' will only get you so far."

"But that's fine," Murdo piped up. "I mean, I know I'll never be as amazing as you or the Great Scot or anyone like that, and I know I'll never be asked to join the Adventure Squad or have my own cartoon series. I might not even get my own fan club. But I can live with that, really I can!"

"Ah, see, that's the thing, though," Cap said solemnly. "I've been in this business a long time, lad, longer than I like to admit. I've spent years going from one life-or-death situation to another and in that time I've seen a lot of superheroes come and go. But here's the thing I've learned: if you don't quite have what it takes, boyo... if you don't quite measure up... the next life-or-death situation you're in might be your last... If you catch my drift?"

"What are you saying, Cap? That I should just stop? That I should give up on my dream?"

Captain Scotland sighed. He suddenly looked very tired and very old. "Just think about this, son. And I mean *really* think about this. If I hadn't stopped that hairy beastie today, if I hadn't arrived when I did for whatever reason... you'd more than likely be dead now, along with everyone else in St Andrews. Am I wrong?"

Murdo thought long and hard before answering. "You're not wrong. But being a superhero's all I've ever wanted to be! It's all I know!"

"Ach, but you're young, laddie. You've got your whole life ahead of you. Please, for your own sake, give it some thought, eh? Goodness only knows I've had my fill of burying young wannabes... Your heart's in the right place, lad, but you're no superhero."

OUCH.

More depressed than he'd ever felt in his short life, Murdo made his way home, where he was warmly welcomed by his loving mother... Or not so much.

"You cannot be serious! What do you mean 'you forgot' to go to the pharmacy? You went out specifically to go to the pharmacy! What on Earth have you been doing all afternoon? For goodness sake, Murdo, do I have to do *everything* myself?!"

"The perfect ending to another perfect day in the perfect life of the spectacular SLUGBOY," Murdo muttered, as he trudged dejectedly upstairs to his room.

EVIL RATING 💀💀💀

HEIGHT (CM) —
178 (AS JAMES MACDONALD);
274 (AS THE TARTAN TERROR)
INTELLIGENCE — 4

STRENGTH — 62
SPEED — 36
FIGHTING SKILLS — 20
BAD BREATH — 100

BIO

James 'Jimbo' MacDonald worked in the Irn Bru factory in Forfar, until the day he fell into a vat of the closely guarded secret ingredient and underwent an RBT (radical biological transformation): he turned into a fuzzy tartan rage monster!!!

It's your typical Dr Jekyll / Mr Hyde deal: whenever MacDonald drinks an Irn Bru he transforms into the Tartan Terror and goes on a good old-fashioned rampage.

The Terror's never had any discernable motivation for causing chaos; there's no end goal in sight, like becoming rich or ruling the world, he just seems to enjoy causing complete and utter devastation wherever he goes.

I guess it's nice to have a hobby.

The Terror's fur is incredibly dense and protects him from serious injury. It's also waterproof, so that's handy (particularly in Scotland). And while the Terror is a sluggish beast most of the time, he can move at high speeds when he draws his arms and legs into his body. In this spherical form, he can steadily build up speed by bouncing against hard surfaces, a bit like a rubber ball does.

The Terror's downfall often comes as a result of his sheer stupidity, like the time Arnold Armstrong lured him into the world's biggest mousetrap with a really huge lump of cheese. True story.

AWESOME RATING POW POW POW POW POW

HEIGHT (CM) — 198
INTELLIGENCE — 98
STRENGTH — 70 / 97
(AS THE RAMPANT LION)

SPEED — 66 / 95 (AS
THE RAMPANT LION)
FIGHTING SKILLS — 87
PATRIOTISM — THINK OF
THE HIGHEST NUMBER
YOU CAN THEN ADD 10!

BIO

Captain Scotland is the embodiment of all that's
great about Scotland. Drawing his powers from
the land itself, he battles evil wherever he finds it
with his magic bagpipes and sporran.

The ultimate expression of Captain Scotland's
great power is when he turns into the Rampant
Lion, a mighty primal beast, invulnerable and quick
as lightning. As with all magic, however, such a
dramatic transformation comes at a price. Cap can
only remain in this form for a limited amount
of time, and upon reverting to his human form
he's left powerless, unable to call upon any of
his magic. This weakened state has been known
to last anywhere from a week to a whole month.

Fun fact: Captain Scotland isn't a
natural redhead. His PR guy thought
he'd have more international appeal
if he conformed to stereotype,
so he dyes his hair!

TRIVIA

Some have theorised that,
because his powers are
so intrinsically tied to his
homeland, Captain Scotland
might lose his powers should
he ever leave the country.

20.
TO BE OR NOT TO BE, SLUGBOY
THAT IS THE
QUESTION

West Lomond is the highest hill in Fife, and it's sort of in the middle of nowhere, so you'd think it would be a nice quiet spot to visit, especially on a dreich Monday morning. That's what Murdo was hoping for when he trudged up there in his Slugboy garb – some peace and quiet.

Murdo's mood was as grim as the weather. He sheltered under an old golf umbrella, wrapped in his cape, thinking about everything that had gone on (or gone wrong) over the last few weeks. This, he thought, was what grown-ups refer to as 'alone time' – sitting and contemplating big questions like: What is the meaning of life? Are we alone in the universe? And is it true cannibals don't eat clowns because they taste funny?

Murdo's mum had often told him that, when it comes to making big decisions, it's important to spend some alone time mulling it over, considering all of the possible consequences or outcomes. And when it came to decisions, they didn't come much bigger than this one: *Should I give up being a superhero?*

Faced with the sickening success Maximum Velocity had achieved in a relatively short space of time, contrasting that with his own successive failures, and taking into account the career advice he'd received from Arnold Armstrong, Murdo had begun to wonder about throwing in the towel. In comic books the heroes never give up, but Murdo seemed to have caused more harm than good since becoming Slugboy. And then there were Captain Scotland's parting words of wisdom, still floating around in his head...

"Penny for your thoughts?"

Murdo leapt into the air. *Those* weren't Captain Scotland's parting words! He turned to find that, despite being high on a damp hill in a remote part of deepest, darkest Fife, he wasn't as alone as he'd thought.

"Psychic Sally! What are *you* doing here?"

"Ice skating! You?"

"What?"

"I'm kidding. I actually came up here for some peace and quiet, but you've obviously *ruined* that plan..."

"Oh, sorry, I can go—"

"Kidding. Again. Not much of a sense of humour, huh?"

"Less and less these days."

"Oh wow, someone call the Depression Police and lock this guy up already."

"You think this is funny?"

"Do you see me laughing? I'm trying to cheer you up, Murdo."

"Yeah, well, thanks, but—

WHOA THERE!

Wait just a minute! You... you called me Murdo! That means you know who I am. But how?! When did...? What if...? How come...? Great prancing polar bears, this is a disaster!" Murdo's mind was racing faster than a toupee in a hurricane. "This is shocking! It's horrific! Worse than that, it's a **CATASTROPHE!**" he whined, pacing round and round. "No one's supposed to know who I am! What if my dreaded arch-enemies find out? Or what if – oh boy – what if my mum finds out?!"

"Relax, Murdo," Sally said, "I'm not going to tell your mum."

"Holy smokes!" Murdo blurted, surprised to find Sally was still there. He'd almost forgotten about her amid his hysterical outburst. "But how did you...?"

"Find out your identity? I'm telepathic, Murdo. I hear people's thoughts. There's a not-very-subtle clue right there in my superhero name."

"But you can't just go around poking your nose into people's heads – you have no right! It's called a 'secret identity' for a reason!"

"I know, and I'm sorry. I didn't mean to pry, it's just... it's not something I can switch on and off, OK? I hear what people are thinking – constantly! All day, every day, I have other people's thoughts running through my head, like I'm at a football match and people are shouting and cheering and singing all the time, and there's nothing I can do about it! That's why I come here – to get away from other people and all that noise. Besides the occasional hill walker, and a distressed superhero or two, it's normally pretty peaceful. So, that's why I'm here. What's your excuse?"

"If you can read minds then you'll already know."

"True. But sometimes it helps to talk about your problems. I read that in a book, so it must be true. Everything written in books is true."

"You want me to talk about my problem? Fine! Here it is: I'm useless. I'm worse than useless – I'm the worst superhero, ever!"

"And you're sure about that, are you?"

"Of course I am!"

"Uh huh... You ever heard of a hero called Mr Nobody?"

"Who?"

"Exactly. His power was to blend into crowds and become instantly forgettable. He's not exactly going to be saving any worlds anytime soon with that lame power."

"Please. I would kill for that power right now, so then everyone would forget how hopeless I am."

"Oh boy, this isn't going to be easy. OK, how about the Human Hair Straightener?"

"What? No way! Someone actually called themselves that?"

"Duncan McIntyre. He can heat up his fingers to scalding temperatures. And no, the name wasn't his idea – I think he wanted to be known as Furnace Fingers, but the name didn't stick. Neither did his superhero career. He's a hairdresser now, has a nice place in Glenrothes. He might even be able to do something with that greasy mess you're sporting."

"That's unbelievable." Murdo giggled.

"Puts things into perspective, right?"

"Are there any more?"

"Are you kidding? I can do this all day."

And that's exactly what she did. Well, not all day, but for an hour or so. Murdo was soon laughing so hard that tears rolled down his cheeks.

Before long, Murdo started opening up about his doubts and fears. It was good to be able to talk to someone about these things. And it was nice that someone finally knew his secret identity, too, especially when that someone was Sally. She was kind and understanding and a good listener. And she was very pretty...

"Focus, Murdo," Sally warned.

"What?"

"Just be careful what you think around me, OK?"

"Oh, right. Gotcha!" Murdo replied, blushing.

"Anyway, back to your problem! You have to learn not to be so hard on yourself, Murdo. Everyone has to start somewhere. Take Dynamo Dave, for instance. He'd never admit it, but he didn't exactly have the world's most successful debut."

"What do you mean?"

"Well, you can never tell another living soul, but Dave started out as Arnold Armstrong's teen sidekick."

"He did? But I thought Arnold had only ever had one sidekick, and that was some hopeless, scrawny, accident-prone kid called... Oh, no way!"

"...Daring Dave!" Sally said it at the same time Murdo did, and they both fell backwards laughing.

"You can never tell him I told you," Sally laughed. "He'd never speak to me again! Not that he says much at the best of times..."

"Your secret's safe with me," Murdo chuckled.

"Say, you wouldn't happen to like a game of **Bottom Trumps**, would you?" Sally asked, once she had regained her composure.

"Are you kidding?" Murdo beamed. "I love **Bottom Trumps**! I never leave home without a stack of them! Mostly because they're handy for telling me stats about all the superheroes and villains I meet on my adventures, but also just in case I'm challenged to a game by some glamorous psychic on top of a mountain!"

"Then prepare to be challenged, Slugboy!" Sally

declared, pulling a stash of cards from her utility belt.

"You're on!" Murdo replied, pulling his out from inside his boot.

"Eww! You keep them in your boot, next to your cheesy feet? I'm not touching those!"

"Oh, grow up! And my feet aren't cheesy, they're lovely!"

"Yeah right, whatever you say, Cheesy Feet..."

For those of you not in the know, here's an incredibly quick guide to playing **Bottom Trumps Heroes and Villains**:

Players sort their cards into two piles: HEROES (blue) and VILLAINS (red).

Each pile is shuffled and then placed face down, in plain sight of all players.

The youngest player begins the game by pressing the spring-loaded spinner, which indicates whether they will select a HERO CARD or a VILLAIN CARD.

If the player in control of the game uses a hero card, their opponents must all select villain cards, and vice versa.

Without seeing their opponents' cards, the player in control decides on a category, e.g. strength, speed, intelligence, etc. Whichever player has the top score in this category wins the hand and takes everyone else's cards. Control of the game then transfers to that player.

Please note that some cards have special:

Unusual Ability Scores

which can be utilised against certain modes of attack.
The instructions for these can be found on the back of
each pack.

Play continues until such a time as players have run
out of cards or it's past their bedtime, whichever comes
first. The player with the most cards at the end of the
game is

Hope that clears that up! Now on with the game!

21.
THE HILLS
ARE ALIVE WITH
THE SOUND OF ~~MUSIC~~
CARD GAMES

Murdo was younger than Sally, so he had first go. The spinner arrow whizzed around and landed on 'villain'. The first fiendish foe from Murdo's villains pile was Captain Cold Front, who produces areas of low pressure (he makes the weather cold). Sadly his ice-attack score of 35 was useless against Insulation Man's unusual ability score of 65 for durability. The first hand went to Sally.

The next spin saw Sally produce a hero card. She drew Arnold Armstrong.

"I have a strength score of 90," she said smugly, knowing full well that there weren't many villains who could top that.

Murdo swiped his top card dramatically from the red deck. "Aw, nuts."

"What?"

"*Oatmeal Man.*"

"Ha!"

That was two rounds for Sally, zero for Murdo.

The game continued a while longer, until Murdo drew one of his last villain cards:

MAJOR DISASTER.

Sally felt Murdo's mind racing but couldn't pinpoint what was going through his head. "What is it?" she asked.

"It's nothing. You'll think I'm being crazy."

"I think that anyway so you might as well tell me."

"OK, fine, but you asked for it, remember. The thing is, all of the villains I've met over the past few weeks have been far more powerful than they're supposed to be. Brodie Brainwave's always used his powers on tiny animals, but suddenly he's able to control a gigantic sea monster! When I fought Daddy Longlegs in Edinburgh, he was twice the size he used to be, and the Tartan Terror was faster – and he could breathe fire! It was like they'd been upgraded somehow, but I couldn't figure out how they'd done it or what connected them.

"Then, when I was on the Loch Ness Monstrosity with Maximum Velocity, he told me all about how Major Disaster had tried to combine mechanics with people and animals to make them faster or stronger or whatever, so I got to thinking, maybe he's done that to Daddy Longlegs and all the others. Plus, when I was helping Captain Scotland the other day in St Andrews, the streets were overrun by cyborg rodents – the same ones I saw in Loch Ness!

"It's all connected somehow, I know it is, I just can't figure out the big picture. Why, after all these years, would Major D start powering up random villains? What's he after? And how is this all connected to the sudden increase in superhuman criminal activity?"

Murdo expected Sally to dismiss his theory straightaway and tell him he was bonkers, but she took her time considering his ideas before she responded.

"It's a sound theory, Murdo – and I'll definitely look into it – but Major Disaster isn't involved."

"How can you be so sure?"

"Because I know exactly where Major Disaster is and I know exactly what he's doing, which isn't very much."

"You do? But how?"

"A few years ago, Major D approached us – the Adventure Squad, that is – saying that he was tired of the supervillain lifestyle. He'd had enough. He wanted to hang up his costume for good and focus his energies on giving his kids a proper childhood, away from lasers and cyborgs and things. But he needed our help. See, he was an escaped criminal, wanted in just about every country around the world. People would never stop looking for him, never leave him alone, unless we pulled a few strings for him. So we found him a secluded little spot on the Isle of Skye, and he's been living out his retirement there ever since."

"So you actually helped him?" Murdo asked, astonished. "Why would you do that? The guy's pure evil!"

"Murdo, think about it. The most powerful supervillain of all time was offering to give it all up in return for a clean slate. I mean, just look at the stats on his **Bottom Trumps** card: he beats every other card in the pack, hands down. By agreeing to his terms, we were saving lives. And if we'd said no, what then? It's not like there was ever a prison that could hold him anyway."

"What about that new super-prison where they keep sending all those villains, THE SLAMMER?"

"Oh, shoot, that reminds me. I'm actually visiting THE SLAMMER tomorrow, but I still need to email them my RSVP."

"Why are you going there?"

"A whole bunch of us have been invited to go see the place. It's a publicity thing, really, but Captain Scotland's meant to be coming, and the Astonishing Saltires, Arnold Armstrong, the Flying Scotsman, the Old Man of Storr... It should be a good laugh!"

"Wow, that's like every major superhero in Scotland!"

"I know, right? I'm totally taking a selfie with Captain Scotland! Anyway, I had better go get in touch with them before they score my name off the guest list, but I want you to promise me that you'll not make any hasty career decisions until we get another chance to talk about it, OK?"

"OK, I promise."

"Good. And don't worry about Major Disaster. The Adventure Squad has eyes and ears on his island. We monitor him around the clock. If he were ever to try anything, we would know about it."

"Cool. That's a big relief, actually."

"Glad I could be of service! Take care, Murdo! I'll see you later."

"Bye, Sally."

Well, would you believe it? Murdo actually had a good day! That's a first. But something tells me it won't be long before things take a turn for the worse...

AWESOME RATING POW POW POW

HEIGHT (CM) — 163
INTELLIGENCE — 78
STRENGTH — 26

SPEED — 30
FIGHTING SKILLS — 45
STAR SIGN — ARIES

BIO

Psychic Sally's something of an oddity among superheroes.
Her powers aren't the result of an accident or an experiment gone
wrong. She doesn't have alien DNA or any cybernetic enhancements
using technology from the far future. Nor has she been injected with
some sort of super soldier serum. No, Sally was born with her power.
She's somehow able to access areas of the brain that lie dormant in
most people. Some have theorised that she might be the next step
in human evolution. Others have suggested her abilities are a genetic
abnormality. One or two people think she's a fluke, like maybe
she was dropped on her head as a baby and her brain somehow
got mixed up on impact.

However it happened, she's telepathic, which is extraordinarily
rare. She can read minds, project her thoughts into people's brains,
and even influence a person's actions for a short period of time,
though this takes considerable effort.

Sally became the youngest-ever member of the Adventure
Squad when she joined at the age of fifteen, but quickly set
about establishing herself as an invaluable asset to the Squad's
never-ending quest to rid the world of evil. She is now one of
the most financially marketable superheroes in Scotland, boasting
a host of corporate sponsors and her own line of sportswear.
Sally also founded Super Sprogs, a children's charity that supports
underprivileged kids.

YET ANOTHER OMINOUS INTERLUDE

It was an epic gathering of heroes, the likes of which had never been seen! Well, not since last year's Christmas night out.

> The Adventure Squad!
> The Astonishing Saltires!
> Captain Scotland!
> Arnold Armstrong!
> The Flying Scotsman!
> And the Old Man of Storr... (Who's cooler than he sounds, by the way – he's made of rock!)

These modern-day titans had been invited to **THE SLAMMER** to see first-hand where their defeated foes were being imprisoned... but some of them had more pressing issues on their minds.

"Lunch is provided, right?" asked one of the Astonishing Saltires.

"Methinks the invitation did speaketh of a buffet," said another one, who did speaketh ye Olde English for no discernable reason.

The heroes were led to a holding area to await the arrival of the world's media.

"Your comfort is very important to us," explained the efficient-looking young lady who'd greeted them at the entrance, "so if there's anything we can do to make your wait less arduous, our attendants will be only too happy to provide you with something from our full range of services, be it a head massage or a computer game, a newspaper or a packet of Wotsits: you name it, we'll find it for you. Then, once you've fed the journalists a few stirring quotes and they've taken all the publicity shots they need, we'll give you a full tour of the complex."

The heroes entered a wide passageway lined with rooms on either side.

"We've taken the liberty of preparing individual dressing rooms for each of you to enjoy while you're waiting. The first room on the left-hand side is yours, Mr Armstrong."

Arnold found a large basket of muffins waiting for him, and two massive dumbbells on either side of the basket. "I love muffins and dumbbells!" He beamed. There was also a full-length mirror and a range of hair products.

"The next room's for you, Mr Scotsman."

"Please, call me 'Flying'," said the Flying Scotsman.

All the heroes were over the moon with their rooms. Captain Scotland's quarters were kitted out in tartan and had a vinyl recording of Jimmy Shand's favourite squeezebox tunes accompanying a repeat broadcast of Scotland's famous 3–2 victory over Holland from the 1978 World Cup.

Aqua Lass found a pile of magazines and books about marine life waiting for her, along with some *Blue Planet* DVDs. "Wow, these guys have obviously done a lot of research on us!"

"Oh, you don't know the half of it," the guide said, showing one of the Astonishing Saltires into the last room, where there was shortbread and a book of Scottish myths and legends waiting.

When the superheroes had all settled happily into their quarters, the guide approached a computer console at the end of the passageway and spoke into a microphone.

"I hope you're pleased with your rooms, ladies and gentlemen," she said over the tannoy system, "because you're *never leaving them ever again!*" Before anyone could react, the guide flicked a switch that activated invisible energy barriers across the front of each room, sealing the heroes in. They were trapped, and soon realised that their powers were somehow being sapped, too!

But who could have planned and carried out such a sinister plan? Where were all the villains who were supposed to be locked in the cells that now held the heroes? And what is the capital of Croatia? Answers on a postcard, please!

END OF
OMINOUS INTERLUDE

22.
DOG-DAY
AFTERNOON

It was the hottest day of the summer. People were having barbeques, dusting off their buckets and spades for visits to the beach, lathering on factor-50 sunblock and soaking up rays in their back gardens.

Murdo, however, hadn't been enjoying any of these things. He'd chased a purse-snatcher around the town centre, the blazing sun beating down on him, only for the thief to be floored by the friendly neighbourhood postman, who just happened to be passing by. Murdo wasn't best pleased. It's bad enough when another superhero turns up and saves the day; being upstaged by a civilian... that's pretty pathetic, even by SLUGBOY standards!

He arrived home dragging his feet, dripping with sweat, puffed out and fed up. "Lousy, poor excuse for a superhero..." He shuffled down the hall and let out a deep sigh as he traipsed into the kitchen.

His mum was rushing around with her hair in curlers, somehow applying lipstick whilst simultaneously hooking on a pair of large, looping earrings that she saved for special occasions.

"Nice day dear?" she asked while putting extra tissues in her handbag and squirting on enough perfume to fill a bathtub.

"Oh sure," Murdo replied half-heartedly. "Super!"

He glanced listlessly around inside the fridge, not really sure what he was looking for but appreciating the cool air nonetheless. "Where are you going?" he asked from inside the fridge.

"Oh Murdo, don't tell me you've forgotten! I've told you so many times!"

Murdo thought hard. He imagined his memory was an Olympic-sized swimming pool and he dived straight into the deep end. After a bit of splashing around, though, he came up empty-handed. "Uh, Zumba?"

"The special workshop for aspiring writers being held at the university, remember?"

"But you're not an aspiring writer – you got published years ago."

"Well yes, that's why I've been asked to share some of my experiences in a panel discussion alongside some very big names. It's all really rather exciting!"

Murdo was pleased his mum was looking forward to her event, but he wasn't terribly interested in books, not unless they were comic books. Or books about comics. Or books about well-meaning, good-hearted, up-and-coming Scottish superheroes that were set in

174

St Andrews. Those ones were good.

Oh, and he liked *Harry Potter*, of course, because everyone likes *Harry Potter*. "Will the *Harry Potter* lady be there?" he asked hopefully.

"No, dear."

"Will there be any comic-book writers?"

"No, dear."

Murdo returned his attention to the fridge. "Bo-ring," he muttered under his breath.

"What was that, dear?"

"Nothing, Mum. That sounds great."

"Yes, well, there's bolognaise in the freezer for your dinner."

I hate Italian food, Murdo thought.

"And my mobile number's on the fridge."

I can recite your mobile number backwards, in Polish, while standing on my head and cutting my toenails.

"And Mrs Parker's next door if you need anything."

Mrs Parker's a hundred years old and she's of no use to anyone, unless there's some sort of knitting crisis, and even then her usefulness would depend entirely on how long she could stay awake...

"And don't stay up too late."

You'll be home by nine o'clock. You're always *home by nine o'clock.* "See you later, Mum! Have fun!"

175

Once his mum had left, Murdo found a tin of beans in the cupboard and dropped some bread into the toaster. As he stirred his beans, he reflected on the traumatic events of the past few weeks: making a fool of himself in front of the Adventure Squad in Dundee; almost letting Daddy Longlegs escape with the crown jewels in Edinburgh; taking a back seat to Maximum Velocity in Loch Ness; and being overwhelmed by a handful of household pets in St Andrews.

Psychic Sally had tried to lift his spirits, but after another disappointing day Murdo silently, sadly conceded defeat. Aqua Lass had been right all along. He really was the world's worst superhero.

He was just about to settle down gloomily to his dinner when, out of nowhere, a translucent, floating head appeared before him. This was the first time a floating head had ever appeared out of thin air in Murdo's dining room, so it came as quite a shock. Naturally he reacted with all of the grace and composure you'd expect: by falling backwards off his chair and battering his bum on the tiled floor.

"Get up off the floor, Murdo," commanded a familiar voice. A girl's voice...

"Are you here about the overdue library books?" Murdo asked sheepishly from under the table. "Because I meant to bring those back..."

"Get up, you great ninny!"

Murdo snuck a look over the edge of the table and

instantly recognised the floating head of his most trusted ally.

"Psychic Sally? What are you doing here? Why can I see through you? Where's your body?"

"I'm using my telepathic powers to project my thoughts directly into your brain," Sally explained. "I'm also tricking your brain into seeing something that isn't really there, hence the floating head."

"Astral projection!"

"That's the one," Sally smiled, but her smile was strained. She looked exhausted. "As for what I'm doing here... I need your help, Murdo. *We* need your help."

Murdo listened intently as Sally explained what had happened at **THE SLAMMER**: how all of Scotland's top superheroes had been trapped, leaving the mastermind behind the evil scheme completely unopposed.

Sally looked wearier by the second as she recounted her harrowing tale, but when she finished all Murdo could say was, "So... I was right?"

"What?"

"I was right. About... everything! The enhanced villains, the increased number of arrests... I actually figured it all out. Me!"

"I think you're missing the point, Murdo..."

"No! Don't take this away from me! This is a rare moment of pride and I'm going to milk it and enjoy it for all it's worth!" Murdo launched into a victory dance that looked like a cross between an awkward goal celebration and some sort of bizarre one-man conga line. "I'm going to frame this and put it on the wall! I mean, I actually cracked this case wide open! Me!"

"Murdo, please, the power dampeners in our cells are designed to restrict physical abilities, like invulnerability or laser blasts or shape-shifting, but they're taking their toll on my telepathy, too. I don't know how much longer I'll be able to maintain this link with you, so you have to listen very carefully: *We need you to save us.*"

"Wait. What?"

"Murdo, all of Scotland's premier superheroes are trapped. Our powers are being suppressed. We have no idea what's planned for us, or how long we'll even be allowed to live! And if we don't make it out... if Major Disaster really is behind all of this somehow... Murdo, the whole planet could be in danger! You have to get us out of here!"

"You're not serious? Listen, Sally, all I ever do is make things worse. I'm a walking catastrophe! I couldn't even catch a stupid purse-snatcher this morning. How am I supposed to save a bunch of world-class superheroes from the biggest Big Bad in history?"

"Man up, Murdo! We need SLUGBOY! Now push that brilliant belly button of yours and get your bruised butt over here, or I swear on Captain Scotland's kilt pin that I'll plant so many frightening nightmares in your subconscious that you'll never get a good night's sleep ever again for as long as you live!"

"OK! All right already... Geez. You can be really scary sometimes, you know that? And you sort of just reminded me of my mum..."

23.
THERE'S METHOD IN MURDO'S MADNESS

THE SLAMMER was built on the Isle of May, a small island in the Firth of Forth. To save Sally and the others, Murdo would first need to make a short journey to Anstruther Harbour. That seemed pretty straightforward. From there he would have to navigate a few kilometres of choppy waters to get to the island. This would probably be a bit more challenging, but it was definitely doable. Then all he had to do after that was break into the most advanced maximum-security super-prison ever created, battle through whatever dark forces he encountered there, defeat the biggest Big Bad the world had ever known, and free all of Scotland's top superheroes.

Hmm.

Let's focus on one problem at a time, shall we? First stop: Anstruther.

It was too much of a strain for Sally to monitor Murdo every step of the way, but she had promised to check in on him occasionally. Half an hour into his epic mission, she did exactly that.

"Murdo... Where are you?"

"I'm at the bus station."

Sally took a deep breath. "Why are you at the bus station, Murdo?"

"Because I'm waiting for a bus."

"You're waiting for a bus?"

"Yep."

"I see. So every superhero in the country has been captured by some ruthless megalomaniac, and the one person who might be able to save us, our only hope for survival, is waiting for a bus?"

"Uh... yeah. It should be here any minute."

"*Are you completely insane?!* Order a taxi! Hire a helicopter! Walk if you have to! Not that I want to rush you or anything, but this *is* an actual honest-to-goodness *life-or-death situation!*"

"Relax! I have a plan. Or at least I have the beginnings of a plan. I haven't quite worked out all the kinks, but it seems to be coming together quite nicely so far."

"Oh, you did *not* just tell me to relax..."

"Sally, my head's feeling sort of crowded at the minute. Could you clear out of there for a little while? I need some room to think."

"You're kidding!"

"Not kidding. Please, Sally, you need to trust me."

"...Fine. I just hope you know what you're doing."

"Yeah, you and me both..."

Despite the urgency of his task, Murdo remained surprisingly calm as his bus rattled along. It wasn't like him at all. Let's not forget, this is the boy who couldn't handle looking after his neighbour's pet rabbit.

So what's behind his sudden transformation? Well, I'm no mind-reader, so I can't be completely sure, but I have one or two (or maybe four) theories:

It might have been due to the fact that he hadn't had time for a drink or for his dinner, so he was delirious from dehydration or hallucinating from hunger.

It could have been because he was suffering from heat stroke. Us Scots don't cope well with sudden heatwaves – we're not used to it – and it was still scorching as Murdo's bus approached Anstruther.

Maybe he'd cracked under the pressure and was having some sort of mental breakdown!

Or perhaps Murdo had actually learned something from his earlier ordeal in Dundee, when he'd dashed off to fight the scaly country-music-loving monster. On that day, as you'll recall, he expended masses of nervous energy during his journey, before sprinting to the city centre as fast as he could, then sliding up the side of the Caird Hall at his top speed, completely exhausting himself before he could do any good. By adopting a gentler, more relaxed approach to this adventure, he'd arrive at **THE SLAMMER** with plenty of gas still in the proverbial tank, ready to save the world feeling cool, calm and collected.

When Murdo reached his destination at 6.15pm, Anstruther was hoaching with people in shorts and t-shirts licking ice-cream cones and enjoying the sunshine. He made his way to a nearby pier and looked across the water to the Isle of May. **THE SLAMMER** stood there in plain sight, a huge dark blemish on an otherwise picturesque view. The sky was clear, the sun still hot, but there was a cool, gentle breeze wafting in from the water.

"Perfect," Murdo said to himself.

After having a quick word with an elderly fisherman who was unloading his gear, Murdo walked to the beach, where he made a large arrow out of stones and shells. Then he turned around, walked off the beach and entered Anstruther's world-famous fish and chips restaurant.

Psychic Sally's head appeared suddenly, like a cartoon light bulb being switched on, but Murdo had been expecting her so didn't fall off his chair this time.

"Murdo, what on *Earth* are you doing? There's no time for you to sit down to a nice dinner! Lives are at stake!"

"When you arrived at THE SLAMMER, were there lookouts posted along the prison walls?" Murdo asked calmly.

"Yes, there were guards patrolling all over the place. What's that got to do with anything?"

"It has everything to do with, uh, everything else. Don't worry, Sally – I have a cunning plan. And it's not a silly plan this time, like riding the trams in Edinburgh looking for trouble, or wading into a sea of monsters in St Andrews armed with nothing but a golf club and an endless supply of pluckiness."

"I suppose those chips are part of this magnificent plan?" Sally asked suspiciously, as a waitress laid a basket of golden, delicious-looking chips on the table.

"Oh yes," he replied. "My whole plan hinges on these chips. Tell the others not to worry. Help is on the way!"

Sally harrumphed, then vanished.

And so, without further ado, Murdo courageously tucked into his towering pile of scrumptious mouth-watering chips.

By the time Murdo exited the chippie a short while later, the wonderful weather had turned grey and cold. People in shorts shivered as they sped past, clutching their ice creams in trembling fingers.

Psychic Sally appeared before Murdo once again.

"What happened?" she asked. "Where did the sun go? Did Major Disaster try to snuff it out again?"

"Nah, it's the haar," Murdo replied, "a thick fog that's very particular to the east coast of Scotland. It always creeps in at around this time on sunny summer evenings and it *always* catches people by surprise." He smiled, tapping his nose. "Local knowledge, that."

"And now you can get to the island without any of the lookouts spotting you through the fog!"

"Exactly! Not a bad wee plan, eh?"

"So far, so good. But how will you find the island now that you can't see anything? And how are you going to get here?"

"Don't worry, I've got it all under control. Follow me!"

Murdo led Sally's floating head to the beach, where they found his arrow made of stones and shells pointing out towards the sea. Next to it was a battered old rowing boat.

"I managed to persuade a kindly old fisherman to let me borrow his boat. He didn't believe me when I said it was to save the world, so I told him I was trying to impress a girl instead and he said I could have it for as long as I needed it."

"You're trying to impress a girl?" Sally asked. "Anyone I know?"

"Um, no," Murdo blushed. "Anyway, that's how I'll find **THE SLAMMER**," he continued, gesturing towards his arrow. "It's in that direction, five miles off the coast, so it'll take me a while to get there. Will you guys be OK in the meantime?"

"Well, we don't have much of a choice, so yeah, I guess we'll have to be. Oh, and Murdo? I'm sorry I doubted you. I'm actually really impressed."

"Yeah, well, don't go getting all proud just yet. There's still plenty of time for things to go horribly wrong!"

24.
THE SLAMMER

The first thing that struck Murdo when he arrived at **THE SLAMMER** was the wall. Literally. It was so misty that he didn't see it coming and he row, row, rowed his boat right into it! There was an awful crunch and his little craft – hardly the most seaworthy of vessels to begin with – immediately sprang a leak. Murdo leapt onto a rocky ledge at the base of the wall and listened for anyone who might have heard the crash, while the fisherman's poor wee boat slowly sank and disappeared from view.

He waited there for a whole nerve-shredding minute, but there was no sign of movement from above or below, and no sounds from within the prison. It seemed as though he'd got away with his carelessness – this time.

Might not be so lucky next time, Murdo thought to himself as he began sliding up the wall. *Must be more vigilant. And slightly less clumsy, too. Might go a long way to increasing my life expectancy...*

Scaling the prison's high, grey wall was proving

pretty problematic. It was made of some kind of slick, polished material that was difficult to stick to, and every so often there were jagged steel spikes jutting out of it. Plus visibility was poor, so Murdo had no idea how much further he had to go, but he persevered, took his time and maintained his concentration.

Finally he heard voices and realised he had nearly reached the top. He risked a quick peek over the edge of the battlements then ducked down at once. There were guards all over the place, just like Sally had said. Murdo slid left and right looking for another entrance, but the building didn't have any windows he could sneak through.

Some rescue mission this turned out to be. How am I supposed to get everyone out of there when I can't even get inside?

He took a few deep breaths to calm himself down then considered his options:

1. Go up and over the wall. This was risky because he might be captured or zapped by the guards.

2. Go through the front door. This was more risky because he would definitely be captured or zapped by the guards.

3. Um... those two options were actually the only ones he could think of...

No, wait! There IS another option! Well, kind of...

"Sally? Can you hear me?" Murdo whispered as loudly as he dared.

Sally's floating head flickered into view, slowly this time. It was faint, slightly out of focus, and she looked much more tired.

"Just... barely. Not sure... how many more times... I'll manage this..." she said with considerable effort. "Strain becoming... unbearable."

"Sorry Sally, but I need to ask a wee favour..."

Moments later, Murdo clambered over the wall in full view of half a dozen muscle-bound goons, all of them armed to the teeth with samurai swords, axes, chainsaws, spears and laser assault rifles, but they were far too busy braiding each other's hair and reciting poetry to take any notice. As Murdo reached the top of a long narrow staircase, one of the guards – a huge hairy guy covered in tattoos – skipped past singing 'I'm a little teapot'.

"Wow, Sally, you did a real number on these guys," Murdo said. The 'wee favour' he'd asked Sally for was to telepathically distract the guards so he could sneak past. He'd suggested projecting something utterly bizarre into their brains, like a four-armed pink elephant playing air guitar while bouncing on a pogo stick, but clearly Sally had had her own ideas. "Remind me never to get on your bad side!"

"Sally? Are you there?"

There was no response.

That last stunt must have used up what little energy she had left, Murdo thought as he started down the staircase. *From this point onwards, I guess I'm on my own...*

When Murdo reached the bottom of the staircase, he stepped out onto a round platform suspended in mid-air, with walkways leading from it in different directions over a gaping chasm. He glanced over the railing, down into what seemed to be a bottomless pit.

The platform was part of a humongous underground complex. Murdo wasn't sure how he was supposed to find the trapped superheroes without Sally guiding him, so, after a bit of thought, he decided to employ a highly scientific method for choosing a walkway – eenie-meanie-miney-mo. Then he crept cautiously over the chasm and entered the complex through a *Star Trek*-style sliding door.

Once inside the prison, Murdo was pleasantly surprised to find that there wasn't much in the way of security, probably because no one was expected to make it over the wall in the first place. *Either that or the Big Bad blew his budget decorating the place, so couldn't afford any more goons-for-hire.* Whatever the case, it was one less thing for Murdo to worry about – and he had plenty of other things to worry about, so that was good!

There were some exceedingly helpful signs by stairwells that described what was on each floor of the prison, like the signs you find in big department stores. Murdo was on Level 25, which housed the armoury, the shooting range and the gymnasium. He ran his finger down the other floors. The living quarters and the mess hall were on Level 20. Level 16 had a dance hall, the infirmary and, rather surprisingly, a crèche (but then I suppose even supervillains need childcare). Level 12 sounded cool – it had a cinema, a casino, an arcade and a sports bar with big screen TVs!

I wonder if all the superheroes are trapped there, Murdo thought hopefully, but he decided they were more likely imprisoned on Level 0, in the holding cells. There was also something called the War Room on that level, which didn't sound very inviting, but Murdo had a job to do and he wasn't going to let something mysterious and ominous-sounding stand in his way.

To anyone else, climbing down twenty-five flights of stairs would probably have been quite hard work, but Murdo simply slid down the middle of the stairwell. Sliding down walls was much easier than sliding up them, so it wasn't too tiring.

When he reached Level 0, it quickly became clear that there were a lot more security personnel down here.

Murdo took that as a cheerful sign he had probably picked the right floor to find the imprisoned superheroes. Luckily there were several storerooms and cupboards dotted around for him to duck into when necessary. Not that he was scared of one or two measly goons, but if anyone sounded an alarm it would be game over. A couple of times when there'd been no way of getting around the guards and nowhere to hide, Murdo had slid up the wall and travelled silently along the ceiling, over their heads, an idea Maximum Velocity had given him while inside the Loch Ness Monstrosity.

If I get out of this alive, I'll maybe Tweet him a thank-you message.

Murdo was following signs to the holding cells when he heard a handful of henchmen heading his way. He instinctively ducked into what he thought was another cupboard without stopping to read the sign above the door:

Murdo watched through the crack in the door as the henchmen moseyed on by.

"Phew," he said, "that was close."

"It's about to get a lot closer, bonehead," said a rasping voice behind him.

Murdo froze. It was probably unrealistic to hope that he'd stumbled into the sports bar...

25.
THE WAR ROOM

Murdo's mind was racing. He didn't know what room he'd stumbled into or who that was behind him with the raspy voice, but he knew he had to get out of there – and fast!

"Um, did someone order a pizza?" he asked, not daring to look.

"Do you even have a pizza?" the raspy voice replied.

"Err, now that you mention it... not so much! I must have left it upstairs. Silly me! If you'll just excuse me for two seconds, I'll go get it."

Murdo made to open the door, but an all-too-familiar metallic hand slammed hard against it, keeping it tightly closed. "Oh come on," he told himself, "how bad can it be? Just turn around and face the music!"

When he turned around, Murdo found he was in a large, dimly lit room. In the middle of the room was a long, thin table. And seated around the table were... a whole host of cheerleaders! Nah, only kidding, sorry! It was actually a bunch of supervillains, sitting together as if they were attending the most ridiculous, dysfunctional, night-marish family reunion ever.

BRODIE BRAINWAVE, the mind-controlling scoundrel who the Adventure Squad had defeated in Dundee, sat on one side of the table, surrounded by a cluster of cute kittens that were under his mental control. Next to him was *DADDY LONGLEGS*, the vile villain who'd almost overcome Arnold Armstrong at Edinburgh Castle. He was wearing a new exoskeleton suit, far more fitted and compact than the egg-armour he'd had on when Murdo had clashed with him in the capital. His new suit was equipped with smaller versions of his mechanical arms and legs, one of which he was using to keep the exit firmly shut. That's why the hand on the door looked so familiar – it was identical to the one that had swept Murdo aside in the castle vault that day and nabbed the crown jewels.

Further down the table was the *TARTAN TERROR*, the fuzzy fiend who'd battled Murdo and Captain Scotland in St Andrews. Thankfully he was in his human form for the moment, but he didn't smell any better (ugh). On the other side of the table were **CHAOS KING**, *Gail Force*, *Captain Cold Front*, OATMEAL MAN and Porridge Princess. All of the villains were wearing 'Hi, my name is' nametags. They were munching their way through handfuls of marshmallows and slurping steaming hot chocolate from novelty mugs.

And in the shadows, sitting at the head of the table

in a grand, throne-like chair, was a dark figure Murdo couldn't quite make out. He was large and bulky and seemed to be wearing armour, the edges of which occasionally caught the light. He was clearly in charge, too, because he had a huge plate covered in sugary doughnuts all to himself and a strawberry milkshake in a tall glass that said:

Number 1 Evil Genius!

"Get a little lost did we?" the dark figure asked, cracking his fingers.

"Not at all," Murdo replied, trying to sound as confident as possible over the sound of his knees knocking together. "In fact, this is exactly where I want to be because... because..."

Loads of reasons for his being there popped into Murdo's head, but the words caught in his throat as the dark figure leaned forward into the light and Murdo got his first clear sight of him. He was wearing a red-and-purple suit of steel-plated armour, with a shiny red helmet that concealed his face. That infamous armour was unmistakable – it belonged to Major Disaster, the most notorious supervillain the world had ever known – and suddenly every inch of Murdo's body screamed 'Run away!'

"Is this someone's idea of a joke?" the armoured figure asked, looking along the table at his motley crew of criminal companions. No one answered, so he returned his attention to Murdo. "Did one of these goons put you up to this? Whoever it was could've at least shelled out for a decent costume!"

"I'm not sure this is a joke," said Brodie Brainwave. "This thrown-together, shoddy-looking misfit looks awfully familiar..."

"I get that a lot," Murdo replied. "I've just got one of those faces, you know? Anyway, I didn't mean to interrupt your meeting, and clearly this isn't a good time for you, so—"

"Wait a minute, I know who this guy is!" Longlegs smirked. "He's that boy off the loo-paper advert!"

"I hate those adverts!" the Tartan Terror barked, slamming his fists on the table. "Can I eat him, boss? Can I?"

"I'm not in any loo-paper adverts," Murdo interrupted. "Do you mean to tell me that none of you recognise me? No one here at all?"

The only response was blank looks from around the table.

"Oh, come on! Tartan Terror, we fought each other three days ago. Three days! How can you not remember me?"

The Tartan Terror scratched his head and frowned. "You're that little twerp who was helping Captain Scotland in St Andrews?"

"That's right!" Murdo said (a little too proudly). "And Daddy Longlegs, I foiled your plot to steal the crown jewels! How could you possibly forget that?"

"You're that nincompoop who opened the vault for me?" Longlegs asked.

"The one and only!" Murdo puffed out his chest. "And Brodie Brainwave, I was there in Dundee when the Adventure Squad thwarted your attack on the city, remember?"

"Nope."

"Really?"

"I have no clue who you are, sorry. Please accept my humblest apologies."

"Oh, um, sure... Thanks."

"So how come you keep turning up to all these things?" the Terror asked. "You some kind of superhero groupie?"

"I'm not a groupie!" Murdo snapped, adrenaline rushing through his veins. "I'm a SUPERHERO! Yeah, that's right, and I know all about your little plan, too. And I'm going to bring it crashing down around you!"

"Got it all figured out, have you, sport?" the Terror snorted.

"Of course!" Murdo boasted.

"So who's the guy at the head of the table, smarty pants?"

"Um... Major Disaster?"

"Ha! What a loser!" Oatmeal Man laughed with a mouth full of marshmallows.

"He's not the only loser round here, biscuit boy," muttered Porridge Princess.

"What did you call me?"

"You heard!"

At which point the pair of them started bare-knuckle boxing (did I mention those two used to be married?) and the other boneheads cheered them on.

"Get her, Oatmeal Man!" called Captain Cold Front.

"Squash that blowhard," said Gail Force.

The only person who refrained from cheering was the armoured figure at the head of the table, who glared at Murdo, eyes narrowed. Then he raised his hand and everyone froze. Not literally – he didn't have ice abilities or time-freezing powers or anything – but they all shut up and stopped squabbling immediately in response to his silent signal.

"You're that little dweeb who ruined my Loch Ness Monstrosity." The armoured figure pointed his armoured finger at Murdo. "You and your speedy wee gal pal, Maximum What's-his-name."

"So it was *you* controlling that machine!"

"Yep. It was something to do to pass the time. You got a name, pinhead?"

"They call me SLUGBOY."

"Who's 'they'?"

"Um... well, there's me, and Psychic Sally called me it once or twice. Err... and some other people, too, like all twelve of my followers on Twitter..."

"Wow, I didn't realise you were such a big deal," the figure replied in mock adulation, which got a chuckle from his marshmallow-guzzling companions. "So I take it you're here to try and save those other spandex-clad numbskulls?"

"I am."

"And how do you propose to do that, Snailguy? The odds aren't exactly stacked in your favour."

"For the freedom of those superheroes, I challenge you... to a game of rock, paper, scissors!"

The assembled villains all went "Ooooh" and turned to their leader expectantly.

"Don't be ridiculous. I'm not risking all my hard work on a game of chance."

"Aw, what's the matter? Are you too chicken?"

"Ooooh," the villains said again.

The armoured figure shuffled uncomfortably in his chair. "...Fine. One game. Winner takes all. Ready?"

"Ready."

"One... two... three... go!"

Murdo held out two fingers in the shape of a pair of scissors. His opponent thrust his fist forward.

"Ha! Rock beats scissors," the villain sneered.

"Two out of three?" Murdo offered meekly.

"Nah, I'm bored with you already," the armoured figure said, rolling his eyes. "Longlegs, if you would...?"

Daddy Longlegs let go of the door and grabbed Murdo with his powerful robo-hands.

"OK, Terror, you can eat him now..."

26.
THE BEST-LAID SCHEMES O' MICE AN' MANIACS

Things weren't looking good for Murdo. He was trapped deep underground in a room full of supervillains. Daddy Longlegs had him pinned to the spot. And the head honcho had ordered the Tartan Terror to eat him. The situation seemed hopeless.

Unless...

"Wait!" Murdo called, turning to the armoured figure at the head of the table. "Um, sorry, who are you?"

"Insufferable child," Brodie Brainwave spat. "This is the mastermind who has single-handedly vanquished every superhero in the entire country, who will go down in history as one of the greatest minds of our time, who will rise from the ashes of Scotland to become King of the World and master of all he surveys!"

"So... Major Disaster?"

The figure groaned and shook his head. He cracked his fingers then pressed a button hidden under one of the steel plates on his armour. Two-by-two the plates shifted down and along until the armour stood open.

The dark figure stepped out from the suit of armour into the light, heaving off the shiny red helmet that concealed his face, finally revealing the brains behind this diabolical operation.

Murdo sniffed. "I'm sorry, I realise this is a bit of an anti-climax, but I genuinely have no idea who you are."

The figure who had exited the armour was a scrawny kid, no taller than Murdo, with spiky black hair. He had dark rings under his pink, watery eyes, but other than that he didn't look particularly menacing. He actually looked incredibly out of place standing next to the colourful collection of over-the-top supervillains.

"I am pain," rasped the kid through a mouthful of squint teeth. "I am darkness. I am a waking nightmare, a relentless, unfeeling engine of destruction. I am the son and rightful heir of Major Disaster, and my name is...

minor disaster!"

A few of the villains sniggered quietly at his terrible name.

"Shut up!" he told them. "And kill this loser already. His whiny voice irritates me."

"Aren't you going to explain your sinister plans before you kill me?" Murdo asked.

"What possible difference would that make? Either way, you'll be just as dead."

"Sure, but don't you want to, you know, show off a little bit? After all, you've obviously put a lot of time and effort into this evil endeavour – seems a shame not to brag about it."

"Well, it *did* take a fair bit of forward planning..."

"Don't fall for it," Daddy Longlegs warned. "He tried the same routine with me, playing for time until Arnold Armstrong came along and saved him."

"Armstrong's not in a position to be doing that again anytime soon," Disaster said.

"Exactly!" Murdo agreed. "And it'd be a real shame to just kill off your arch-nemesis without explaining your plan!"

"You're not my arch-nemesis. Are you even a real superhero?"

"Of course I am! Anyway, it's like you said, I'll be just as dead either way, so you might as well enjoy recounting the tale of how you captured all of Scotland's top heroes, right?"

"Well, when you put it that way... Prepare to be terrified by the terrific tale of Minor Disaster's terrible triumph!"

"For years people thought Dad was the meanest, scariest, most fearsome villain of all time, but to me he was the greatest hero that ever lived, always attempting to take over the world with one of his awesome inventions, or hatching a flawless plan to topple corrupt governments."

"Hold up," Murdo interrupted. "How could he be a hero if he kept trying to take over the world?"

"Because he believed that if everyone on the planet was united under one ruler, then instead of always fighting and arguing with each other we could all work together, ushering in a golden age of peace, the likes of which has never been seen."

"Ah, OK. Carry on."

"Thank you! So, Dad was a great man, who worked tirelessly for the betterment of mankind, but time and time again those lousy, no-good, spandex-clad hooligans spoiled his noble efforts."

"Wait. Stop, please," Murdo said. "First of all, 'betterment' isn't a word. Secondly, are you seriously trying to tell me that Captain Scotland and the Adventure Squad and all those other superheroes – who've saved the world from alien invasions and time travelling megalomaniacs and prehistoric, man-eating, fire-breathing, country-music-loving monsters – are actually villains?"

Disaster sighed. "Not in the traditional sense, no, because they aren't evil, per se, but they *are* a bunch of misguided morons who probably can't tie their own shoelaces, much less begin to grasp the complexity of Dad's wonderful schemes. All of the incredible contraptions they've ruined over the years, all the gadgets they've destroyed... marvellous machines designed to advance technology for the good of all!

"My whole life I watched Dad's dreams being torn to shreds and trampled. I watched as his spirit dwindled and his will to win was squashed, until he finally gave up all hope for a better tomorrow and retired from the spotlight. These days he's a shadow of his former self, a broken man who wastes his brilliant brain watching TV box sets and playing 'Sonic the Hedgehog' with my little sister. And gardening. He loves gardening.

"As his only son and heir, I decided that I couldn't let Dad's efforts be for nothing – I had to pick up where he left off and achieve his goal of world domination!"

"World domination for the betterment of mankind...?" Murdo asked.

"What? Oh yeah, sure, whatever. Anyway, I figured that if it hadn't been for these so-called 'superheroes' always interfering, no one would have foiled his well-laid plans, so I got to thinking, *How can I take them out of the equation?* And I mean *all* of them. Capturing one or two heroes would be child's play, but to trap them all... that would take some doing! I needed to concoct the ultimate plan... Which I obviously succeeded in doing because here we are, so well done me!"

Disaster stopped to take a long sip of strawberry milkshake (explaining crucial background information is thirsty work). He stuffed a jam doughnut into his mouth and then continued, spraying sugar as he spoke.

"Over the course of his long and glittering career, Dad was wrongfully imprisoned about twenty times, but no jail could hold him. He escaped every time, each breakout more brilliant and cunning than the last. Instead of telling me bedtime stories when I was little, Dad used to describe to me in detail how he'd broken out of each of the prisons. Ah, memories..." Disaster said dreamily. "It was those very stories that inspired me to create

THE SLAMMER.

"I thought a lot about the different ways Dad had escaped, thought about the flaws he'd exploited and what could be done to stop it from happening again. And so I designed **THE SLAMMER**, the perfect prison, from which no one will ever abscond. That means 'escape'," Disaster added, noting the confused look on Murdo's face. "All I needed then was to lure those miserable, rotten heroes here. That's where *these* loathsome creatures came in." Disaster gestured to the villains sitting around the table. They didn't seem to mind being referred to as 'loathsome creatures'. One or two of them actually looked quite pleased with themselves. "I call them my 'Criminally Insane Posse of Doom'. Came up with the name myself."

"Wow."

"I know."

Minor Disaster cracked his fingers again and continued. "Using everything Dad had taught me about biomechanics and genetic modification, I upgraded each of these idiots in return for their services (such as they are), making them more powerful than ever."

"That's how Brodie Brainwave was able to control that massive monster in Dundee," Murdo said. "And why Daddy Longlegs was so much bigger when I confronted him at Edinburgh Castle. And the Tartan Terror's new fire-breathing ability..."

"Yep, all down to me." A smug grin crept across Disaster's face. "I sent them to cause havoc up and down the country. When a worthy opponent showed up to stop them, they allowed themselves to be captured and were sent here, where they awaited the final, glorious step in my master plan.

"**THE SLAMMER** was hailed as an incomparable success: over a dozen supervillain incarcerations and counting, with no escapes or attempted breakouts. I simply waited for the inevitable media frenzy to build and then invited those dim-witted super-buffoons for a visit. Superheroes can't resist a buffet and a bit of good publicity, so they came in their droves, only to be locked up by yours truly.

"With all of Dad's greatest adversaries caged like animals, there's no one to stand in my way. All that's left to do now is launch my attack on the Scottish Parliament Building. Once I've seized power, Brodie Brainwave will use his augmented abilities to force the First Minister to sign over complete control of the government to me.

"First I'll conquer Scotland, then the rest of the UK

And after that... the world!" Disaster laughed his most evil laugh, a high-pitched cackle that would have made any wicked witch proud. He laughed so hard and for so long that eventually he gave himself hiccups, making him seem slightly less menacing.

Once he had his hiccups under control, Minor Disaster said, "And there you have it," looking very pleased with himself. Then he waited. He waited to see the look of unmitigated terror sweep across Murdo's face as the sheer brilliance and magnitude of this inspired plot sunk into his puny mind. He waited to hear him howl and scream and beg for mercy, to curse the name of Disaster and yell, 'You'll never get away with this!' But those words never came. In fact, no words came at all.

An uncomfortable silence lingered as the seconds ticked slowly by. Murdo didn't say or do anything. He hardly moved at all. His cheeks were becoming quite rosy and a few beads of sweat glistened on his brow, but that was hardly the melodramatic response Disaster had been expecting.

"Lost for words, are you?" Disaster demanded. "Stunned into silence by my brilliant braininess?"

No reply.

"Now you're just being rude," Disaster whined. "Say something!"

"Can't," Murdo replied. "I'm concentrating."

As I may have mentioned once or twice already during this breathtakingly epic superhero saga (that you *will* recommend to your friends, yes, you will), our Murdo has two distinct superpowers. One is sliding up walls. He uses that power a lot and it's in no way unhygienic or disgusting. His other power is the weird ability to become all horrible and slimy, which is much less cool, a lot more disgusting and pretty much useless... until, perhaps, now.

All the time Minor Disaster was bragging about his cunning scheme and Daddy Longlegs was holding him in place, Murdo had been focusing on producing as much of his greasy gunk as he could. Now loads of the fine, oily goo was oozing out of his pores. It slid down his arms and covered Longlegs's massive mechanical mitts, slithering in between his fingers, making them slippery... and allowing Murdo to squirm free!

27.
SLUGBOY VS. THE CRIMINALLY INSANE POSSE OF DOOM!

Before he swallowed a radioactive slug and became **SLUGBOY**, Murdo had always dreamed about being a superhero. He'd imagined going on exciting adventures in exotic locations; pictured saving the world from rotten wrongdoers. There was never any real danger, no possibility of failure, because the good guys always won. Now that he was on the biggest adventure of his life, however, it didn't feel like a dream come true. This was more like a nightmare.

Murdo knew he was no match for the combined might of the Criminally Insane Posse of Doom, so the instant he slid from Daddy Longlegs's metal grasp he sprinted out of the War Room, stopping only to smear a great wad of goo on the floor outside the door. As he charged down the corridor, he glanced over his shoulder to see Captain Cold Front slide on the slime patch and fall on his face.

"Sweet! Maybe this slime thing isn't such a lame

power after all!" Murdo cheered, but his happiness was short-lived, as the rest of the villains poured out of the War Room, leapt over their fallen comrade, and started chasing after him!

Daddy Longlegs and the Tartan Terror led the charge. The Terror must have guzzled a sneaky Irn Bru, because there he was in all his red, green and blue-furred glory. He had drawn his arms and legs into his fuzzy body and was ricocheting off the walls like a giant, hairy bouncy ball. Daddy Longlegs, at the same time, had extended his robotic arms to within two centimetres of catching the fleeing Slugboy.

If he had stopped to think about the insurmountable odds he was facing, Murdo might have given up by now. Luckily he wasn't the type to stop and think, so instead he did something extremely brave (or insanely stupid): he hit the brakes abruptly and ducked under Longlegs's robo-hands, then jumped onto the speeding Tartan Terror as the furball bounced by, snatching two big handfuls of tartan fuzz and clinging on for all he was worth.

Don't worry, he hadn't gone completely loopy. He'd remembered his Loch Ness adventure, when Maximum Velocity had used his enhanced speed to tangle up the Monstrosity's tentacles. Murdo obviously wasn't as fast as Max, but the Terror had been building momentum with every bounce along the corridor, so was bounding along at a pretty impressive speed.

The Terror can't come out of his ball shape in these tight corridors without colliding painfully with a wall, Murdo thought, *so he's stuck like this for the time being. If I pull on his fur with all my might, I should be able to steer him like a giant space hopper and, with a bit of luck, that'll take care of Longlegs's pesky artificial limbs...*

"Stay still, you fool," Longlegs said, frantically trying to catch Murdo and the Terror. He sent his arms from side to side and weaved them in and out, but Murdo kept one bounce ahead of him, turning the Terror this way then that. Round and round Longlegs went, until his arms got completely tangled and hung there helplessly. Murdo bounced onwards, whooping and cheering. He guided the Terror towards the freight elevator then let go of his fur, diving off just as the furry fiend bounced inside. Murdo bashed the button:

sending the villain to Level 25.

"That's two down," Murdo said, but before he could find his bearings or work out how many villains were left, Oatmeal Man and Porridge Princess rounded the corner and unleashed their oatmeal launchers. Murdo dodged the sticky spray and avoided Oatmeal Man's granola grenades, then retreated round the next bend and ducked into a cupboard filled with cleaning supplies.

He held his breath until the two breakfast-themed thugs had thundered past.

When it had quietened down, Murdo emerged from his cupboard and followed the signs to the holding cells. Unfortunately, he found the formidable female, Gail Force, guarding the entrance. As her name suggests, Gail could generate gale-force winds, simply by huffing and puffing with her superhuman lungs (maybe Big Bad Wolf would have been a better name).

"End of the line, kid," she boasted, sucking in an enormous lungful of air. Murdo reacted quickly (first time for everything). He charged at Gail, who steadied herself for an attack, but then he hit the deck, skidding along the ground like a footballer going in for a sliding tackle. Still oily and slippery, Murdo slid the length of the corridor, through Gail's legs and on towards the entrance to the holding cells. Gail was furious. She unleashed a powerful gust of air, but this only succeeded in propelling Murdo through the entrance.

"Thanks for the lift, windbag!" he shouted, squeezing the door shut and pushing the button:

Murdo was now in a wide passageway lined on either side by cells full of superheroes. There were no iron bars; the barriers holding the prisoners in were made of pure energy.

"And if the barriers are made of energy," Murdo surmised, "there has to be an off switch somewhere."

Arnold Armstrong was in the nearest cell, munching sadly on a blueberry muffin. Seeing him brought back painful memories for Murdo.

'I don't think this whole superhero thing is right for you,' Arnold had told him in Edinburgh. 'You're just not made of the right stuff for this line of work.'

Just wait till he sees that I've come to rescue him, Murdo thought. *Me, SLUGBOY! That'll change his tune!*

"It's you!" Arnold snapped angrily when he saw Murdo. He threw himself against the invisible barrier, causing it to fizz and spark. "I knew it! You've been working with them all along!"

"What?!"

"Why else would you help Longlegs escape with the crown jewels? You're a villain!"

"No, I'm not!" Murdo protested. Suddenly he was seething. How could Arnold think such a thing? For a second or two it crossed Murdo's mind to leave the big idiot here and let him rot... but that was a fleeting notion. SLUGBOY was a superhero. He didn't do that sort of thing. "I'm here to save you!"

"You are? ...OK then, cool. Err, what's your name again?"

Murdo sighed. "My name's not important right now. How do I deactivate these barriers and get you guys out of here?"

"There's a control station at the far end of the passageway. Once the barriers are switched off, we should get our powers back and—"

Arnold was interrupted by a loud thump at the locked passageway entrance. Murdo turned to see a large, fist-shaped dent in the metal door.

"I guess they know you're here, then," said Arnold.

"I guess so," Murdo replied. "Sit tight, I'll have you out of there in a jiffy!"

Murdo ran towards the control station, passing all the superheroes he'd idolised for years. The Flying Scotsman was cheering him on.

He's got 70 for speed on his **Bottom Trumps** *card*, Murdo thought. *Maybe when this is all over he'll give me a few pointers...*

The passageway entrance started to buckle and crack as the thumping continued. It wouldn't hold for much longer.

Bottom Trumps stats churned through Murdo's mind as he sped past Captain Scotland, Aqua Lass and the Old Man of Storr. *68 strength, 20 for speed, fighting skills 18...*

Then the temperature dropped sharply as the entrance turned to ice and shattered into a million tiny pieces.

"Time's up, amigo," Captain Cold Front jeered, admiring his handiwork.

The gaping used-to-be-a-doorway was soon filled with supervillains. Even Minor Disaster had joined the party, flanked by a horde of horrible henchmen.

"You're done for, Snailguy," Disaster teased. "There's only one way into this place and one way out, and that's through us! You're trapped!"

Keep talking, pal, Murdo thought, trying to focus on the control station up ahead as blind panic set in. *Almost there...*

Then Chaos King was standing between him and the controls.

"Aw, nuts," Murdo said. "Since when can you teleport?"

"Surrender now, child," Chaos King growled, "and your death will be quick and painless."

"Wow, what a generous offer! But I might need to use a lifeline before I decide... Can I phone a friend? Ask the audience?"

"Insolent whelp!" Chaos King snarled, swinging his flaming emerald sword. Murdo leapt through the air. He somehow avoided being chopped in half, but the villain delivered a sharp elbow to his stomach and sent him tumbling to the floor.

Winded, Murdo struggled to his feet. He glanced over his shoulder. The control station was right behind him, almost within touching distance, but he had no clue how to work it. Even if there'd been an instruction manual, time wasn't really on his side. He edged backwards as Chaos King advanced slowly towards him.

"I don't suppose you'd like to surrender?" Murdo asked.

Chaos King responded with a guttural roar.

"I'll take that as a no, shall I? OK, tell you what, let's call it a draw and then we can both go our separate ways with our heads held high. What do you say?"

Chaos King lifted his blade above his head. It looked like the end of the road for SLUGBOY ...

28.
PRISON
BREAK

As Chaos King brought his blade down, Murdo squeezed his eyes shut. *If this is how I'm going out,* he thought, *at least I can be proud that I gave it a good shot. I faced off against some of the most powerful villains in the world, even managed to get the better of a couple of them... And for once I didn't slip up and look like a complete and utter idiot!*

Yeah, don't speak too soon, buddy...

Murdo jerked to the side as he felt the heat of Chaos King's sword approach. His heel caught the end of his cape, which tugged at his neck, pulling him off-balance and sending him tumbling backwards.

He slammed into the control station, somehow bashing the right combination of buttons and switches to deactivate the energy barriers, freeing all of the superheroes! Without a moment of hesitation, the Astonishing Saltires lunged out of their cells, tackling Chaos King as one.

"Sweet!" Murdo cheered as more heroes emerged from their cells. "It's payback time, Disaster!"

What followed was an epic, earth-shattering battle.

Arnold Armstrong and Dynamo Dave started wrestling the gruesome twosome, Oatmeal Man and Porridge Princess.

Captain Cold Front and Gail Force combined their powers to freeze Aqua Lass mid-blast. Some of Disaster's henchmen stepped in for the kill, but Psychic Sally disorientated them with one of her patented mind-blasts.

The Old Man of Storr laid into Gail Force, while the Flying Scotsman and Greenfly Guy took on Captain Cold Front. Even Captain Scotland, powerless after his most recent transformation into the Rampant Lion, got mucked in, sorting out a few minions.

While the battle raged on, Murdo spotted Minor Disaster and Brodie Brainwave making a hasty exit.

"Oh no you don't!" he shouted, chasing after them. He'd already defeated a handful of certified supervillains this evening – he wasn't about to let some punk kid escape!

Murdo hurdled over Porridge Princess, stuck to the ground in her own gooey oatmeal, and stooped under Captain Cold Front, who was being swung through the air from his ankles by the Flying Scotsman. Then he was out the used-to-be-a-door, pursuing Disaster through THE SLAMMER.

They're heading for the stairs, Murdo thought. *Awesome! That actually sort of plays right into my hands!*

The villains were well ahead of him by the time Murdo reached the stairs, but he wasn't too concerned. He simply leapt against the wall and started sliding up the middle of the stairwell.

He reached the top of the stairs just behind his quarry and then chased them out onto the round platform suspended in mid-air: the place with the walkways leading in different directions over a gaping chasm.

"Give yourselves up," Murdo called, "and I'll take it easy on you!"

Disaster turned and scowled. "Are you completely mental?"

"That's a matter of opinion! Either way, I'm taking you in, Disaster!"

"Oh please, do you honestly believe you have any hope of defeating me, you pathetic worm? You're nothing more than an insignificant maggot, a gnat waiting to be crushed beneath my boot heel. You couldn't hope to comprehend the true extent of my power."

"...Yeah, you lost me after 'pathetic worm'. Can't you speak like a normal kid for two seconds?"

"But that's the whole point, dummy. I'm not a normal kid. I'm an evil genius!"

"Uh, no, you're *the son* of an evil genius, smart guy. There's a difference."

"You're a real pain, you know that?"

"Ah, now *that* I understood! Anyway, enough small talk. Time for the beating of your life, Disaster!"

"Sorry, but that simply isn't happening; not today. See, you're about to fall into a deep sleep. Don't worry, though – I won't throw you over the edge into that bottomless pit while you're unconscious. No, I've got something much worse planned for you, you miserable little moron. Yeah, you're going to wish you never crossed paths with me, pal."

"What are you talking about? And why would I fall asleep in the middle of—

AAARGH!"

Murdo's ears were filled with a loud, piercing noise that made his head spin and brought him crashing to his knees.

As his vision blurred, the last thing he saw was Minor Disaster, glaring down at him.

"Sweet dreams, Snailguy. I'll be seeing you soon..."

And then the world went black.

When Murdo opened his eyes, Psychic Sally was leaning over him.

"Great crawling caterpillars," Murdo muttered, half-dazed, "you're gorgeous."

"And your brains have been stir-fried," Sally replied, helping him to his feet.

Murdo was dizzy and had a thumping headache. "Did we win? Am I dead?"

"See for yourself."

There were superheroes assembled all around Murdo. They looked delighted to see him up and about, coming over to congratulate him, clap him on the back and shake his hand.

"I don't understand... What happened? Why did I black out?"

"Well, let's start with some good news. Thanks to you, we managed to defeat the so-called Criminally Insane Posse of Doom and we've now got them locked securely in their holding cells."

"What's the bad news?"

"The bad news is that their boss escaped."

"Sorry about that," Murdo said. "I really thought I could take him, but I guess I'm still the same old waste of spandex that I've always been."

"Hey, don't put yourself down. You got knocked out by one of Brodie Brainwave's mental attacks. That could have happened to any one of us. It was a very brave thing you did, going after the Big Bad on your own, and check it out – you're still standing. That's pretty incredible, SLUGBOY!"

"You think?"

"I do. And in recognition of your heroic efforts here

today, I'd like to officially offer you honorary membership of:

THE ADVENTURE SQUAD."

"You're kidding!"

"Nope, not kidding. You've earned this. So, what do you say?"

Murdo took a moment to consider Sally's offer. He thought about his adventures in Dundee, Edinburgh, Loch Ness and in St Andrews. He thought about his failures, but also about everything he'd learned from them, and he made up his mind.

"Thanks Sally... but my answer's no."

Psychics are notoriously difficult to surprise, but Sally was genuinely shocked. "What? I thought this was all you've ever wanted."

"Don't get me wrong," said Murdo, "I appreciate the offer, really I do... but I'm not ready for it. Not yet. I'll become a member of the Squad someday, Sally, but not today – not when I've got so much more still to learn."

Sally seemed to understand. She smiled and kissed him on the cheek.

Well, that decides it, Murdo thought later, getting a lift home in the Adventure Squad's private jet. *I guess I'm not the world's worst superhero after all...*

EPILOGUE

It was a drizzly Saturday morning in St Andrews, the last one before school started back for a new year, and Murdo McLeod – like every other self-respecting schoolboy in Scotland – was still in his bed, fast asleep and snoring his head off.

"Murdo! Are you awake yet?" his mum called, knowing full well that he wouldn't be. "There's a letter down here for you!"

Murdo staggered down the stairs, bleary-eyed. On the small table by the door was a brown envelope with his name and address scrawled across the front.

Inside it was a small piece of paper and what looked to be a single **Bottom Trumps Heroes and Villains** card. Murdo took out the piece of paper first, as that seemed the civilised thing to do. It simply read:

Then Murdo took out the **Bottom Trumps** card and looked at it. He looked at it for a long time, his eyes growing wider and wider, until the world's biggest smile stretched across his face.

"Great kung-fu kicking kangaroos... I did it," Murdo mumbled. "I don't believe it... I actually did it. *I DID IT!*"

AWESOME RATING POW

<u>HEIGHT</u> (CM) — 140

<u>INTELLIGENCE</u> — 26

<u>STRENGTH</u> — 12½

<u>SPEED</u> — SNAIL'S PACE

<u>FIGHTING SKILLS</u> —
  SORELY LACKING

<u>CATCHPHRASES</u> —
  GREAT LEAPING LIZARDS,
  GREAT JUMPING JELLYFISH,
  GREAT RUNNING RACCOONS
  ... THE LIST GOES ON.

BIO

The kid swallowed a bug and now he can slide up walls. Slowly.
  Nuff said.

YAY.

CAN MEGAN AND CAM BEAT THE BAD GUY,
DEFEAT HIS ROBOT TRANSFORMERS ...

... AND BECOME THE SUPERHEROES
THEY WERE BORN TO BE?

 Also available
as an eBook

Loki is unleashed
which spells TROUBLE
for Greg and Lewis in...

Brace yourselves for Norse
mischief and mayhem from
The World's Gone Loki trilogy

 Also available as eBooks

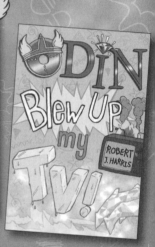

Giant robot chickens are terrorising the city of Aberdeen. Their aim: to peck out all signs of human resistance.

LIFE IN A CHICKEN APOCALYPSE ISN'T ALL IT'S CRACKED UP TO BE